# LEGACY OF LIES

## FOG LAKE SUSPENSE: THE COLSONS

CHRISTY BARRITT

## CHAPTER ONE

INSATIABLE HUNGER GROWLED INSIDE ME, and all I could think about was eating.

Not *just* eating.

I needed something specific to take away the pangs filling my belly. My very life felt like it depended on feeding my need.

It had been too long.

I'd been patient. So, so patient.

But no longer.

I leaned back in the flimsy plastic chair as I imagined the pleasure of getting what I want again.

Drool pooled in my mouth at the thought, and I lifted a napkin to wipe the tangy ketchup from my lips.

Nothing would stop me from satisfying my urgings.

Behind me, men began to yell as a football game played on the TV above them.

I frowned.

Idiots.

They were all idiots.

Unlike me.

I was brilliant, even if other people couldn't see it.

That was okay. Soon, people would realize exactly what I was capable of.

My time was now.

And my hunger was for . . . death.

# CHAPTER TWO

MADISON COLSON SAT up in bed and gasped, trying desperately to force air into her lungs.

Oppressive panic claimed every part of her, and her heart plunged with every beat as her body fought for survival.

Finally, sweet breath filled her. Her panic was met with relief—for now.

But confusion still marred her thoughts.

She blinked, desperate to remember the truth.

What had just happened?

Then it all raced back to her.

A man had broken into the house.

He'd found her in the bedroom.

His hands had circled her throat. The air had

been cut off from her lungs. She'd flailed as she fought to stay alive.

One last wisp of consciousness had filled her before blackness invaded from the corners of her gaze and consumed her.

Then everything had faded around her as death pressed closer.

Madison glanced around the dark room as she remembered how someone had tried to strangle her.

Cold fear formed an iceberg in her chest. Her lungs tightened until she could hardly breathe.

Was he still here?

That's when she heard movement.

*No...*

Overwhelming terror engulfed her, clogging her lungs.

Her heart raced out of control.

She tried to scream. She couldn't.

Instead, she reached for the cell phone charging beside her bed.

It was gone.

"How did you like that little trip I sent you on?" The man's eerie voice caused another ripple of terror to rush through her.

Then his shadow appeared before her.

He'd been watching her the whole time, hadn't he?

She tried to scoot back in bed, desperate to get away. But her body didn't cooperate. Fear paralyzed her despite the adrenaline racing through her system.

He'd killed her, hadn't he? Then he'd somehow brought her back to life.

*No, no, no, no . . .*

This couldn't be happening.

But Madison knew it was.

"They always say that death brings fresh perspective." The man was standing next to her bed now, a black mask concealing his features. "Do you agree?"

"Why are you doing this?" Her voice came out raspy, her windpipe achy and broken.

"Because it's fun. Everyone deserves to have a little fun sometimes, don't they?" Sickening amusement danced through his voice.

Did she recognize those tones? She couldn't be sure. Nothing made sense.

Madison touched her throat, wanting to protect it. But it was no use.

She was trapped. Cornered. Helpless.

"Please . . . leave me alone." Her voice quivered as her words filled the air. "I didn't do anything to you."

"Yet you did everything."

The next instant, the man was on top of her. His legs trapped her in place. His hands pressed on her shoulders.

Madison kicked, but there was no use. He outweighed her by at least sixty pounds.

"Do you know how thrilling it is to see the last traces of life slip from someone's eyes? It never fails to remind me of how fragile life is."

He liked watching people die?

"Please." Her voice cracked.

"It's okay. Don't fight it. There's no need to draw this out."

"You don't have to do this." Her voice sounded hoarse and desperate, but she didn't care. None of that mattered.

Only staying alive did.

He ran his finger along the side of her face. "Oh, but I do. I'm so glad you decided to come home to Fog Lake, Madison."

The next instant, his fingers clutched her neck again. Their pressure dug into her windpipe. Made her eyes feel like they bulged. Made her heart stutter.

She tried to pull in another breath of air.

But it was no use.

She couldn't.

As lights flashed in her eyes, she clawed at his viselike grip. She kicked her legs. Tried to scream.

But nothing changed.

All she could see were the man's eyes above her. The satisfaction in their depths.

He was enjoying this.

He was . . . sick.

As if to confirm the thought, his deep laughter filled the room. "I'm not done playing with you yet, Madison. Not at all."

She clawed at his hands one more time, desperate for air. Desperate to stay alive. Desperate not to delve back into the depths of terror she'd experienced as death had claimed her only moments earlier.

Her body convulsed as if it knew what was coming, as if it wanted to fight for every last second.

But it didn't matter.

Madison knew this was the end.

"DID YOU SEE IT?"

Special Agent Shane Townsend looked up as his partner walked into his office at the FBI field office in Knoxville, Tennessee. "See what?"

Agent Brammall practically shoved Shane aside as he set his laptop computer on the desk and crouched in front of it. He fiddled with the keyboard a moment before pressing something and stepping back. "Watch this."

Shane hoped this interruption was worth it because he'd been in the middle of writing up a report. The task was necessary, but one of his least favorite things to do. And any interruption by rookie agent Brammall generally annoyed him. The man was a little too eager and entirely too talkative.

Shane leaned closer to the screen as the video began playing, curious as to what the big deal was. He hoped Brammall hadn't overhyped it.

A man with some type of wearable action camera appeared to be jogging down a wooded road in the evening. His steps slowed when he spotted something on the shoulder of the road.

"What's that?" the man muttered.

His steps then quickened, the camera bouncing as he ran toward the object.

Not an object.

A *woman*.

She lay collapsed by the roadside, a heap of clothing and outerwear.

"Oh, no . . . what happened?" The jogger knelt beside the woman.

As her face came into view, Shane noted the petite woman was probably in her late sixties, with wrinkling skin and gray hair piled in a beehive.

The jogger checked for a pulse, then slapped her face.

"Ma'am, wake up," he ordered.

But she still didn't awaken.

He placed his hands over the woman's heart and began CPR. "Stay with me. Stay with me."

After several minutes of chest compressions, the woman's eyes sluggishly pulled open, and she turned her head as she tried to focus.

"Oh, thank God!" the man said. "You're okay! You're okay!"

The woman moaned.

"I'm going to get you some help," the man muttered.

Then the camera faded to black.

The title of the video was *Good Samaritan Saves Woman After Heart Attack*. The setting appeared to be mountainous and lush, more like the Appalachians than the Rockies. The leaves were turning the colors of autumn, leading Shane to conclude this had been shot recently.

He leaned back, trying to process what he'd just seen and not jump to any conclusions. "Okay, so this guy just saved someone. That's good news, right?"

"The woman in that video . . . her name is Verna Colson." Brammall's voice held barely contained excitement. "According to the report I read, she died of a heart attack three days ago. The same day that video was posted on the internet."

Shane was losing patience. "So, the guy finds her passed out, gives her CPR, brings her back only for her to die en route to the hospital?"

"That's the thing. Local authorities think she had the heart attack while taking a walk through town. Her body was discovered on the roadside by passersby the next morning. This guy," Brammall pointed to the screen, "never called 911."

Shane turned to him, waiting to hear the rest of his thoughts. Clearly, there was more to this. "Okay . . ."

Brammall looked up at him as if he expected Shane to have this figured out. He quickly shook his head and glanced back at the video. "I'm sorry, I thought . . . never mind. Don't you think this is eerily similar to The Good Samaritan Killer?"

Shane sucked in a breath.

The Good Samaritan?

Colson?

The pieces clicked in place.

The Good Samaritan Killer, identified as James Colson, had terrorized the Smoky Mountains nearly fifteen years ago when he'd killed seven women over a four-year period. Colson had pretended to be the hero by saving women from whatever perilous situation they were in, and he'd recorded it all.

However, what the videos didn't show was that he was the one who'd put them in those situations in the first place. After he "saved" them, he would then proceed to kill them, sometimes bringing them back to life yet again before ultimately murdering them for good.

The man was sick.

But he was also behind bars.

Shane hadn't thought about him in years.

"Is Verna Colson related to James Colson?" Shane finally asked.

Excitement lit Brammall's gaze. "She's James Colson's sister. She lived in Fog Lake."

Fog Lake . . .

Just the mention of the town brought back so many memories. Memories mostly of the time

Shane's father had spent away from the family as he'd obsessively tried to put a serial killer behind bars.

The sacrifice was for the greater good. That's what his dad had always said.

But Shane's childhood had been more reminiscent of someone with a single mom than two happily married parents. Until the day his father had died, their relationship had remained distant.

Shane kept his voice even. "You think there's a copycat?"

"That's what I wonder."

Shane leaned back in his seat as he processed what his colleague had just told him. "How did you come across this?"

"My sister follows all that true crime stuff. She has alerts set up for . . . well, various things. She found this and sent it to me."

"Have you shown anyone else yet?"

He shook his head. "I came to you first."

"Good. I'm going to talk to Ross and see if we can look into this. I want to get down to Fog Lake and talk to the people there." Shane rose to head to the office of the Special Agent in Charge.

"There's one more thing."

Shane paused.

"It turns out that James Colson's daughter—twenty-six-year-old Madison Colson—just returned to town."

Now *that* caught Shane's interest. "So, Madison returned about the same time all this happened?"

Brammall nodded almost eagerly. "That's right. In my mind, that makes her a person of interest."

Had one of Colson's kids decided to follow in their father's footsteps?

It was a possibility. But the jogger in the video had clearly been a man. Still, Shane didn't believe in coincidences.

Shane nodded toward the SAC's office. "Let me get this approved. Then let's talk to Madison Colson and see what she's got to say."

# CHAPTER THREE

MADISON DRAGGED her eyes open as something pulled her from her slumber.

Her head spun, and everything was hazy around her. Her limbs were heavy. Confusion marred her thoughts.

She smoothed a hand across her forehead, which felt unusually cold.

What had happened? Why did she feel like she had the worst hangover of her entire life?

Nudges of the truth tried to work their way into her thoughts, but she pushed them back. Maybe she wasn't ready to handle the truth.

Then a loud pounding sounded at the front of the house.

Each strike caused her headache to throb harder.

What was going on?

She sat up. Sunlight poured in through the window.

The last thing she remembered it was still dark . . .

At once, memories of last night flooded into her mind.

Her gaze darted around.

The man.

Where was he?

Her room appeared empty.

Madison held her hand out in front of her and moved her fingers. Blinked. Breathed.

She was alive. She couldn't believe it.

That monster brought her back to life again.

But she couldn't remember any of it.

The moment of giddiness turned into a moment of horror.

Her entire body began to tremble.

She touched the side of her arm and felt a tender spot there.

Realization filled her. He must have drugged her.

He'd *wanted* her to survive. To remember what he'd done.

And to live in distress from the fallout afterward.

A cry escaped from deep inside her as tears pressed into her eyes.

Why had this happened? Why?

Her breathing became labored again as she tried to fight panic.

Then the pounding at the front door started again.

"FBI!"

She froze.

The FBI? What was the FBI doing here?

Bad memories from years ago bombarded her.

Should she answer?

Before she could figure it out, a man wearing an FBI jacket peered in her window.

He spotted her. Motioned for her to answer the front door.

There was no way Madison could avoid them now. They'd think she was trying to hide something. They'd come in after her.

She had to talk to them.

Should she even tell them what happened last night?

Madison had zero faith in the system. Zero.

With no choice but to face them, she stumbled out of bed, her wobbly legs barely holding her weight. She fell into the doorframe, catching onto it to prevent herself from falling to the floor.

After drawing in a few ragged breaths, she propelled herself into the hallway, leaning against the wall for a moment as she tried to right herself.

But her head wouldn't stop spinning.

*Oh, God . . . why is this happening?*

She took another step before the contents of her stomach spewed all over the floor.

She stared at the puddle of liquid before taking the edge of her T-shirt and wiping her mouth.

Part of her wanted to sink into the ground and disappear.

But that wasn't a possibility.

"Open up!" a deep voice commanded.

She jumped at the forceful demand.

Her mind raced as she tried to figure out what they were doing here. Had they somehow known she'd been attacked?

If not, should she tell them? Would they believe her? Would they do anything about it?

Or would telling them what happened only bring her and her family more scrutiny?

She didn't have the answers to those questions.

But she'd need to figure out something soon.

Madison grasped the doorknob and braced herself for whatever would happen next.

---

"MADISON COLSON?" Shane stared at the woman on the other side of the door.

He'd seen Madison Colson's picture online, but this woman looked nothing like the demure woman he'd expected to see with long, light-brown hair, an easy smile, and a killer figure.

Her eyes were bloodshot. Her hair disheveled. Her T-shirt stained. Bruises splotched her neck.

Bruises?

Could those be from a fight with Verna?

But it was more than that. Her eyes were glazed with confusion, and she leaned against the door frame to keep herself upright.

He showed her his badge before slipping it back into his pocket. "Special Agent Shane Townsend. This is my colleague, Special Agent Kurt Brammall. We'd like to ask you a few questions."

Madison's hand grasped the doorknob as her haggard gaze locked on him.

She was high, wasn't she?

His gaze went to the side pocket of her black leggings and the bag sticking out from it.

Heroin?

At once, Shane's instincts went on alert.

He pushed past Madison and stepped inside the home of the now deceased Verna Colson. "What's going on here? You need to talk. Now."

She grasped her throat, her gaze hollow as she stared at him. Something unspoken haunted her eyes, making it clear she had secrets she wasn't willing to share.

"No . . ." Her voice sounded raspy.

Without asking permission, Shane indicated for Brammall to stay with her while he began searching the house. He had to know if something was going on here.

Something deadly.

Even worse . . . what if this woman had something to do with her aunt's murder? Sure, the Good Samaritan in the video had clearly been a man.

James Colson was in jail, serving several lifetime sentences. But what if he'd had an apprentice? What if two people were now working together to carry on his legacy?

Until they had some answers, Shane needed to proceed with the utmost caution.

He glanced around the outdated house. It almost made him feel like he'd stepped back into the seventies.

Dusty knickknacks—mostly figurines—cluttered every surface. Avocado and mustard-yellow walls stood as a testament to times past. The scent of cigarette smoke was accented by a nicotine-stained yellow ceiling.

He moved throughout the house, gun in hand in case he ran into trouble. When it came to the Colsons, one had to be careful.

As he stopped by the second bedroom, his breath caught.

Vomit puddled the floor outside the room. A bag of what looked like heroin rested on the dresser along with a syringe. And a bottle of hydrofluoric acid sat on the nightstand.

Suddenly, things made a lot more sense.

He left the room and charged back toward Madison. "We're going to need to take you down to the local sheriff's office."

"The sheriff's office?" Madison's eyes widened, and her voice seemed to seize at the thought. "Why?"

"Can you explain the heroin in the bedroom? In your pocket?"

His questions seemed to roll over her in phases.

"Heroin? ... I ... this ..." She ended with a shake of her head, as if she didn't know what to say.

Shane sensed her excuses coming, but he had no desire to listen. Instead, he took the cuffs from his pocket and pulled her hands behind her back.

"Am I under arrest?"

"You're under arrest for the possession of an illegal substance," he started. "Anything you say can and will be used against you ..."

Shane didn't know what was going on here in this sleepy little tourist town.

But he knew about the deadly legends surrounding it.

Legends dating back more than a hundred years ago when a massacre had occurred along the shores of its cloud-covered lake.

Evil wasn't supposed to be handed down to people. It wasn't supposed to encompass a town.

But what if it did?

# CHAPTER FOUR

THIS COULDN'T BE HAPPENING. She couldn't have been attacked. Couldn't have been arrested. Madison kept repeating those words to herself over and over.

Yet they weren't true.

Everything felt surreal, almost as if she were living someone else's life as she went through the arrest procedures.

The FBI agent—Townsend? She couldn't remember—had taken her arm and escorted her to the backseat of his SUV. No one had been nearby to witness it—only an empty street on the edge of town, one filled with several derelict houses.

Memories of the day her dad had been arrested filled her mind. It seemed the whole town had come out to watch her and her brothers being taken away as their father had been placed in the back of an unmarked sedan. There had almost been a sense of victory in the air.

That day, Madison had felt her entire world shift. She remembered sitting in the back of the car crying and reaching for her dad. She'd been desperate to feel his arms around her. Yet, at the same time, she intrinsically knew there was no going back.

Her childhood as she'd known it was over.

Townsend had taken her to the sheriff's office, explaining she was being charged with drug possession. Then she was booked.

She'd taken her stained clothing and placed them in a bag as directed. Then she dressed in some black sweatpants and a sweatshirt that the deputy had provided. Her top was oversized, so she'd pulled the sleeves over her hands, desperate for warmth.

But it didn't matter what she had on, a deep chill began at her core and spread throughout her limbs.

She was given a drug test. Photographed. Fingerprinted. They even took a DNA sample—a saliva test.

The sheriff's deputy who processed her asked if she wanted medical help.

Madison had said no.

Then he escorted her into a cold interrogation room.

At least they'd removed her handcuffs.

"Is there anything you want to tell us?" Agent Townsend sat across the table from her, his bright blue eyes fastened on her. The man had light brown hair that was cut short and a matching beard and mustache, trimmed neatly.

He was probably six feet tall, and trim in his black cargo pants and long-sleeved FBI shirt.

She could see the determination in his gaze—determination to find her guilty.

The police—feds, law enforcement of any type—couldn't be trusted. They had only let her down time and time again.

Madison said nothing, only stared at Townsend.

He frowned, clearly not appreciating her silence. "You can make this as easy for yourself or as hard for yourself as you want."

She still said nothing.

Wasn't that what her brother told her to do? *Don't talk to the FBI. The feds . . . they twist whatever you say.*

Yet another internal voice urged her to tell them everything.

But why should Madison bother? The feds had their minds made up.

They wouldn't believe her, no matter what she said.

Especially if there was heroin . . .

The monster who'd done this to her must have left the drugs. He must have wanted to play with her mind even more. Had he called the FBI himself? How had he known they would come?

The man was sick. So sick. And now Madison was entangled in his plan.

A hollow feeling echoed inside her. Coming here to take care of her aunt's funeral had seemed hard enough. But now this . . .

The attack. The FBI showing up at her aunt's house. It was too much. Too fast.

It was so hard to believe that the loving, caring father she'd grown up with was now regarded as one of the deadliest serial killers in the US.

More nausea rose up inside her. It had been a long time since that thought had brought that reaction. She'd had almost fifteen years to accept the fact her dad was a killer.

And to accept the fact that a piece of information she'd offered the feds had helped put him behind bars.

She wrapped her arms across her chest as an ache formed.

Instead of answering Agent Townsend, Madison closed her eyes, trying to get rid of the images. But flashbacks from last night filled her.

Memories of waking up in her old bedroom to find the man lingering in front of her.

Memories of his fingers around her neck, squeezing the life out of her.

Memories of the same man bringing her back to life. How many times? At least three. Each time he seemed to delight in it more and more.

A cry escaped from her, and she doubled over, hardly able to handle the emotional trauma battling inside her. She thought she might vomit again, but nothing came up.

It still could.

How was she going to get out of this?

She stared at the man sitting across from her. Townsend.

He seemed all business and no compassion.

That fit what she remembered about those FBI agents who'd come to arrest her father.

They weren't to be trusted.

They'd twisted her words to make it seem like her father was guilty all those years ago.

And Madison had no doubt they'd twist her words again.

---

SHANE HAD TAKEN Madison to the Fog Lake Sheriff's Office. But as soon as the two of them had gotten into the interrogation room, Madison had lawyered up.

He'd had no choice but to leave her in the room until her attorney arrived.

In the meantime, he met with Brammall and Sheriff Wilder.

Sheriff Luke Wilder had an exemplary record for keeping things safe in town. The man had to be close to Shane's age, and his eyes were serious as he listened to Shane explain what had happened.

"Do you know this girl?" Shane nodded through the two-way glass into the interrogation room.

Wilder glanced at her and frowned. "She went to grade school with my younger brother. Seemed like a nice kid. What happened with her father shook up this whole community, to say the least."

"I can only imagine." Shane glanced at the file they'd already put together on her. "Says she started a nonprofit called Blood and Water. She helps people who've had their lives torn apart after family members have committed crimes. She doesn't have a criminal record. Not even a parking ticket. I'm assuming she's just back for the funeral?"

"That's a good guess." Wilder shifted. "You're telling me that Verna's death wasn't a heart attack?"

"That's our working theory. We sent you the link to the video. We think that someone is recreating James Colson's crimes."

Wilder shrugged and ran a hand over his face. "Before word of this gets out, we need to confirm that this isn't just an elaborate stunt. How do we know that's really Verna in the video? Could it be someone who looks like her? Could this whole thing be a setup or a prank?"

Shane nodded. "At this point, we don't know anything for sure. But we're here to help figure this out. We'd love the assistance of your department in the process."

"You'll have whatever you need. This is the last thing we want happening in our town."

Shane glanced back through the window at Madison again.

The woman certainly didn't have the look of a serial killer. Then again, neither had her father.

She probably wasn't doing herself any favors by

not talking. In this case, her silence only made her look guilty. But it was her choice—and her right.

"I have a team at the house right now looking for any more clues," Shane said. "We also took samples from beneath her fingernails to see if anyone else's DNA was there."

Wilder shifted. "Did you notice the bruising around her neck? It's hard to see with the sweatshirt, but I'm nearly certain that it's there."

Shane's jaw twitched. "I saw that also. At first I thought it could be defensive wounds from a fight with Verna."

"They almost look like choke marks, don't they?" Wilder asked.

Shane's heart beat harder. "You're right. They do. There's definitely more to this story. I'm not going to give up until I get to the bottom of it."

His phone rang, and Shane saw it was Brammall. He quickly put the device to his ear.

"We found something I thought you'd want to know about," Brammall started. "On the back door .. . hanging from the knob . . . there was a silver cross."

Shane's heartbeat quickened.

A silver cross?

That was the Good Samaritan's calling card.

# CHAPTER FIVE

RELIEF RUSHED through Madison when Isaac strode inside the interrogation room. Without even saying a word, his imposing presence brought a brief respite from the craziness.

Isaac Colson was the type who owned a room as soon as he stepped inside, the kind whose confidence made him a natural leader. It was more than his towering height, curly brown hair, and toothy smile. He was truly someone others could depend on.

In fact, two years ago, Memphis had experienced severe flooding. A reporter had captured a picture of Isaac carrying an elderly woman through flood waters, from her house to safety. He'd been considered a hero by many ever since.

Madison rose and fell into his arms, so thankful he'd already been on his way to Fog Lake when she called. Otherwise, Madison would have had to wait for him to drive from Memphis—a six-hour trip, if he didn't run into any traffic.

He took a step back and studied her face with a grimace. "You look like the dickens, Sis."

Madison scowled as she lowered herself back into the cold metal chair and muttered a sarcastic, "Thanks."

"No offense intended."

She raised an eyebrow as she nodded toward his outfit. "Well, you look like a million bucks, if that makes you feel better."

Isaac's suit probably cost more than one of her weekly paychecks. His dark hair was held in place with gel. An expensive watch adorned his wrist, and his glossy shoes had probably never seen a piece of dirt.

He'd done well for himself. To look at him, nobody would know his past.

His looks and confidence screamed success.

That had been his goal—to erase the old part of him and reinvent himself.

He'd succeeded.

Pride filled Madison's chest when she thought about how far he'd come.

As Isaac sat beside her, his gaze turned to concern. "What happened? I knew we should have never come back to this place. It's trouble."

Madison stared at the sickly, beige-colored wall across the room and shook her head, not wanting to speak the atrocity out loud. But she had no choice. Not if she wanted her brother to help her.

She touched her neck and felt the bruises stretching there.

Her brother pulled her hand away, and his eyes narrowed as he stared at the discolored skin.

"Madison . . ." His voice held disbelief as if he didn't want to believe what he was seeing.

Another cry started to rise inside her, but she swallowed it. Instead, a gurgled sound escaped her throat, almost as if she were choking.

"It was so horrible." Her words were barely discernible to her own ears, spoken both low and garbled.

Isaac leaned closer. "I can tell. I know it's going to be hard, but you've got to tell me what happened. The feds are holding you on drug charges?"

She ran a hand over her face before picking up the bottle of water and taking a long sip.

"I just got into town yesterday evening. I didn't even think anyone knew I was here. I was only here long enough to grab a few groceries, unpack, and head to bed. The drive from Nashville was taxing, to say the least."

"Go on. Take your time. But not too much time." He glanced at the two-way glass beside them.

His words almost made Madison want to smile. They sounded so much like her brother. He'd always been so honest—painfully so, at times. That's why it had surprised her so much when Isaac became a lawyer, a career where most were perceived as being dishonest.

Last night slammed back into her mind, and she felt herself reeling.

"I woke up, and this man was on top of me. His hands around my throat." Madison shook her head, unsure if she could continue. But she had no choice except to push ahead. "He squeezed my neck until I stopped breathing and passed out. Then he performed CPR to revive me. He did the same thing . . . three times."

Isaac gaped. "Madison . . ."

She shrugged, not knowing what to say. This all seemed like a nightmare she would wake up from. But it wasn't—and nothing could change that fact.

"Why didn't you tell the feds?" Isaac asked.

Her gaze locked with his. "What are they going to do? They're going to find some way to blame me for this. Especially with the drugs . . ."

"Do you have any idea how they got there?"

"My best guess is that that man planted them. But I know what the feds are thinking. They think I'm a druggie. They think while I was high, I did something horrible to someone. They're going to come after me and think I'm following in Dad's footsteps." Fear made her voice tremble.

His gaze locked with hers. "We don't know that."

"But don't we? We've seen this play out before. We know how it works."

"If you don't say anything, they're going to think you're hiding something. Because you are. You're hiding what happened to you, something you have no culpability in."

She lowered her voice. "I don't know if I can trust them. I just don't know anything right now."

Just as when they were eleven and thirteen years old, Isaac grabbed her hand and squeezed. "We're going to get through this, Maddie. One way or another we will."

But would they? Had they really ever gotten through what happened to their father?

Or had they just continued forward because they had no other choice?

---

SHANE LISTENED as Madison sat across the interrogation table and told her story.

Each new detail made his skin crawl, which said a lot considering some of the cases he'd handled.

But if Madison was telling the truth, what she'd gone through was horrific.

"Why didn't you tell us what happened when we showed up at your aunt's house this morning?" he asked.

Isaac stiffened beside her. "My family has a bad relationship with the FBI, to say the least."

Shane heard the bite in the man's words but ignored the tone. "You're saying you have no idea how the drugs got there?"

"My only theory is that whoever tried to kill me left the drugs there, after he injected some into me, to make my life even more miserable if I came forward." Madison's voice sounded fragile, and she continued to rub her throat.

"Who knew you were coming back into town?" Shane asked.

"Just my brothers." Madison's words were soft, and grief made her voice sound thin. "We didn't want to tell anybody. This place doesn't exactly have happy memories for us."

"So, you think this killer was waiting for you to return so he could set his plan in action?"

"I have no idea." Fire suddenly lit Madison's gaze as she turned toward him, almost as if she'd turned her energy from her pain to her distrust of law enforcement. "That's what you guys are supposed to figure out."

Shane heard the accusation in her voice but didn't reprimand her. The woman had been through a lot.

"Are you charging her with anything?" Isaac's crisp, professional voice cut through the air.

Shane remained quiet for a moment, not wanting to seem too anxious to give an answer, until he finally shook his head. This woman . . . she was a victim. She didn't deserve to be treated as a criminal.

"No, we're not. All the charges are dropped, and I'm sorry for the way things played out. I wish you'd explained earlier when we arrived at the house."

Isaac straightened and squared his gaze with Shane. "Speaking of which, can we go back to Verna's house?"

"It hasn't been cleared yet. If you give me a list of anything you need, I can have someone pick it up for you."

"I'll do that," Madison said.

She should still get to a hospital to be checked out, but she'd refused earlier. Maybe her brother could convince her to head there now.

"I know I've already said this, but I highly recommend being checked out by a doctor. We did a tox screen on you but—"

"I'm fine. I just want to forget this happened."

"Madison . . ." Her brother's eyes burned into her.

"Please." Her voice trembled as she shook her head. "I just want to get out of here."

Isaac stared at his sister another moment as if trying to determine her mental state and the best plan for her well-being. Finally, he nodded, still looking unconvinced. "Okay."

"One more thing." Madison turned back toward Shane. "Why did you show up at my aunt's house when you did?"

Shane frowned. He'd been waiting for this to come up. "Actually, a video surfaced that concerned us."

Tension spread through her gaze. "What kind of video?"

"A video of your aunt . . . being found dead and then revived."

"You mean . . ." Madison didn't finish the statement.

Shane nodded. "Just like The Good Samaritan Killer."

Madison went eerily still as tension spread across her features. "But her heart attack . . ."

Shane didn't have to respond.

Madison clearly already suspected the truth. Her heart attack hadn't been natural.

"We need to go," Isaac said, abruptly standing.

Shane's jaw tightened as he realized this opportunity was slipping away. But there would be other chances to talk to Madison—he'd make sure of it. "If I have more questions—and I'm sure I will—I'll be in touch. In the meantime, be careful. Please."

As her brother led her away, Shane's thoughts continued to race. If his instincts were correct, he would end up staying in Fog Lake longer than he'd anticipated.

He would need to find somewhere to stay until he figured out how this atrocity would unravel.

# CHAPTER SIX

"I DON'T LIKE what's going on here," Isaac said as he led Madison outside to his car an hour later.

Someone had first brought Madison a bag full of her clothes and her phone. She'd cleaned herself up some in the bathroom and pulled her hair back into a neater ponytail. A kind woman who worked the front desk had also given her some coffee.

Madison wasn't sure what her brother meant by his haunting words.

"What are you getting at?" Madison glanced up at Isaac as he moved her forward, almost as if desperate to get away from this place.

"Verna's death? Then someone attacks you? And the FBI shows up? It's like a bad repeat of fifteen years ago."

Her blood turned cooler. He had a good point. Madison hadn't even thought about the timing of all this until now.

She paused beside a black Lexus. *Isaac's* black Lexus. Go figure, that was the kind of car he had.

She still remembered when a developer had rolled into town driving one of these when she and Isaac were in elementary school. Isaac's eyes had lit up, and he'd declared that one day he would drive one. In his mind, the vehicle had been the epitome of success.

It appeared he'd arrived.

She took a deep breath and let the midafternoon sun warm her face. The air even smelled like autumn—like crisp leaves and hay bales. Down the street somewhere, she heard what sounded like a street musician singing and playing guitar.

All happy things.

None of which she could relate with at the moment.

Before climbing inside Isaac's car, Madison turned to him. "What are we going to do?"

"We're going to figure this out." He frowned. "And we have to bury Verna."

Verna. Isaac had never been able to call her Aunt Verna. He'd refused to claim her as a relative.

Yet, for some reason, his words caused another round of tears to well in her. Madison generally didn't consider herself a crier. But the trauma she'd endured kept her emotions close to the surface and nearly uncontrollable.

Isaac wrapped his arm around her shoulders and pulled her close. "I'm so sorry, Sis. Did you tell Bear yet?"

Bear? She hadn't even thought about calling her older brother. "I could only make one call. It was to you."

"What do you say we go pay him a visit?"

She stepped back and used the sleeve of her sweatshirt to wipe her eyes before nodding. She tried to ignore the dread that pooled in her stomach at the thought of seeing Bear again—and the possible drama that might bring.

"Okay." She let out a long breath. "Let's go find him."

But she had to wonder if her oldest brother would be happy to see them or not.

He'd texted her and Isaac about Verna's passing, keeping his words matter of fact. But, before that, it had been ten years since they'd spoken.

And their last conversation hadn't been pleasant.

---

"WE GOT THE BLOOD PANEL BACK." Brammall nearly flung himself into the conference room.

Shane looked up from his temporary desk, the conference table, his curiosity spiking. "And?"

"Madison Colson had heroin in her system, along with zolpidem, a sedative."

Shane rubbed his jaw. "So, she was either drugged or she took heroin along with some kind of pill?"

"That's how it appears."

He leaned against the table, letting his thoughts percolate. "I don't know what's going on here, but I don't like it."

Brammall's eyes burned into his. "You think she's innocent?"

"Did you see the bruises around her neck? I believe her when she says someone strangled her and then revived her. My gut also tells me she didn't take those drugs willingly."

"You really think The Good Samaritan Killer is back? That the wrong man was put in jail?"

Shane shifted his jaw as thoughts battered him. "Either that, this is a copycat, or James Colson had an apprentice. That theory was thrown around multiple times."

"What if the wrong guy was arrested?"

Shane scowled. "He wasn't. The evidence against him was irrefutable."

Brammall opened his mouth, almost as if he wanted to refute the claim. But then he seemed to think better of it and asked, "What's next?"

Madison's image filled his mind again—her bruises, her haunted gaze, her pain.

He wanted to make sure he handled this case correctly—no jumping to conclusions, no accusations without proof, no mistakes.

"The sheriff already said we could set up an office here. We need to get organized. Then I need to call SAC Ross again and give him the update. I also want to review Verna Colson's autopsy results, and I want to watch that video again. What if it wasn't Verna but someone who looked like her?"

"I suppose it's a possibility." Brammall paused, his gaze narrowing with thought. "Just curious—how long did James Colson wait between kills?"

"His timeline shortened as he grew more confident. There were eight months between each of the first four victims. By the end of his killing spree, there were mere days."

"That's good news, right?"

Shane locked gazes with Brammall. "Maybe. The problem is, we don't know what number this killer is on now."

His words hung in the air.

But the truth was, Shane's father's legacy depended on finding answers about what was going on here.

And even though he'd had a strained relationship with his dad, part of him didn't want to let his father down . . . especially since his dad was the one who put James Colson in jail.

# CHAPTER SEVEN

MADISON FELT the nerves rattling inside her as the mountain road they traveled became narrower with every turn. Nature seemed to squeeze in on her.

Just like life was at the moment.

She had to concentrate on her breathing or overwhelming thoughts would begin to batter her until she couldn't breathe.

Not breathing wasn't an option right now.

"Where exactly did Bear move?" Isaac mumbled as his hands gripped the steering wheel, and his gaze remained focused on the winding asphalt.

"The boondocks," Madison muttered. "Where he always wanted to live, depending on no one but himself to survive."

"I knew he was a recluse but . . . you think he's totally off-grid?"

"I think it's a good possibility." Madison dragged in a breath as anxiety built inside her. "At least the leaves are pretty."

"At least. And there you go. The optimist in you never dies." Isaac cast a quick smile at her.

She shrugged. "I could say the same about the realist in you. Or, as I like to call it, the pessimist."

"It's not pessimistic—"

Madison raised her hand to stop him before his soliloquy started. "I know, I know."

She'd heard his explanation a million times before. *Pointing out the negative things in life doesn't make a person a pessimist. It makes them a realist. Expecting bad things all the time—that's what makes someone a pessimist.*

"Up until today, how has life been treating you, Maddie?" Isaac glanced over at her.

She shrugged as the past several months played in her thoughts. "I can't complain. I love what I'm doing. Nashville is nice."

"How's the guy?"

"*The guy*?" Madison let out a laugh. "Eric and I broke up six months ago."

Isaac's eyes widened. "What? Why didn't I know this?"

"Because you never call."

He shrugged. "I beg to differ. I called . . ."

"Seven months ago." Her voice trailed. "I only remember because it was my birthday."

Isaac frowned and continued to stare at the road. "Sorry. I'm going to do better."

"I know being a defense lawyer keeps you busy." She didn't fault him for the lack of communication. Being together stirred up so many memories—good and bad.

"What happened with Eric?" Isaac stole a side glance at her.

Memories slammed into Madison's mind—memories she'd rather forget. "I caught him with Layla."

Isaac's eyebrows shot up. "Your best friend, Layla?"

She crossed her arms over her chest. "The one and only. They were in a full lip-lock in his car. When I confronted them, they tried to tell me that Layla had a lash in her eye, and Eric was helping her get it out."

Isaac let out a low chuckle. "That's bull."

"Isn't it, though?" Madison sucked in a deep,

calming breath—in theory. It was time for a subject change. "What about you and Kate?"

An unreadable emotion flashed through Isaac's gaze before disappearing with his shrug.

"Kate? Yeah, she and I are . . . hanging in." Isaac's words didn't sound convincing.

"What's wrong?"

"Wrong? Nothing's wrong." He quickly shrugged again.

Avoiding a question wasn't like him. "Isaac, I know you better than that. Spit it out."

He let out a sigh and ran his thumb across his jaw—another telltale sign of stress. "We're just at that point where she wants more, and I . . ."

"Don't want to commit?"

"It's not that I don't want to commit." His voice sounded strained as he said the words.

"It's that you don't want to commit with Kate?" Madison tried to fill in the blanks.

Isaac let out a breath, and wrinkles seemed to form around his eyes. "It's complicated. Check that GPS again. Are you sure we're headed in the right direction?"

Madison knew a distraction when she saw one. Her brother was avoiding this conversation. Whatever was happening between him and Kate must really be burdening him.

The woman seemed like a bit of a handful, but Isaac was a smart man, perfectly capable of making wise choices—even when it came to love.

She glanced at the GPS on her phone. "It says this is the way there."

The roads climbed higher with every wheel rotation. Trees squeezed in tighter. Guardrails were sparse.

Twenty yards ago, the pavement had ended, turning into gravel.

Now, only dirt lay beneath the tires.

She was surprised Isaac had taken the Lexus this way. An off-road vehicle seemed more appropriate. She could have brought her own car, but the sedan had seen better days. Leaving it at Verna's seemed like a good idea.

Madison only prayed they didn't meet another car on this lane. Not only was there no room to pass —there was also no room to turn around. Uneasiness grew inside her. She'd much rather navigate Nashville traffic than this.

"Oh, Bear . . ." Isaac sighed. "Where are you living?"

Madison glanced around and shivered. The isolation unnerved her. "Good question."

"We just need to get this graveside service over with. Then, in a few days, we can all resume our lives as normal. Coming back to this place was a mistake . . . last night proved it. I'm just sorry you had to go through what you did." His voice softened as he glanced at her.

In some ways, Madison was ready to put this part of her life behind her also. But another part of her needed more closure. Could she really move on without answers? Could she live with herself knowing justice hadn't been served and that innocent people could still suffer?

Before she could formulate her response, a man appeared in the road in front of them.

As Isaac swerved to avoid hitting him, Madison closed her eyes and braced herself for whatever might happen next.

SHANE STUDIED the file Brammall had put together for him on Madison.

She had a squeaky-clean record, almost as if she'd been overcompensating for what her father had done. She'd dedicated her life to her nonprofit. She'd been honored in Nashville for her work and had even been written up in a few magazines.

She appeared to be single, to love country music, and her smile lit up a room.

In her normal life, at least.

Not today.

Shane leaned back in his chair and frowned.

No, today she'd looked like a shell of a person.

Quickly, he typed her name into Google and clicked one of the first links he saw. A video of Madison at a charity event began playing. In it, she wore a black dress that showed off her long, thin limbs and slender shoulders. Her hair had been swept up into a twist of some sort. She smiled as she posed with friends and colleagues by a fountain outside an event center.

People shared with the reporter how wonderful Madison was. How much she'd helped and supported them. How she was truly an example.

He paused the video and stared at her smiling face. Madison Colson appeared to be the picture of sincerity and selflessness.

But someone seemed determined to wipe that grin off her face.

Why?

Shane stood and grabbed his keys. Enough researching. He was ready to do some footwork now.

"Where are you going?" Brammall appeared beside him.

The man had the uncanny ability to sense Shane's every move—a fact that annoyed Shane to no end. "I'm going back to the scene."

"Great. Let me grab my coat. I'll go with you." He scurried across the room to the coat rack and snatched his bomber jacket.

A few minutes later, they were in Shane's SUV heading toward Verna Colson's house.

"I checked with the prison," Brammall said. "James Colson is still there. Madison has been his only visitor over the past month. Otherwise, he hasn't had any letters or emails. Nothing."

Shane stored that information away.

As Brammall continued to chat about football, Shane tuned him out. He'd learned it was easier to do that than to repeatedly ask him for quiet.

Finally, they pulled up to Verna's. The local sheriff's deputy guarding the scene lifted the crime-scene tape so they could enter the residence.

Shane paused just inside the front door, ignoring the scent of flowery perfume, Pine-Sol, and old books.

"What are you looking for in here?" Brammall turned toward him.

Shane raised a hand, motioning for silence. Brammall's ramblings made it hard to think, to concentrate. "Just give me a minute. I want to get a better sense for this place."

"I'll talk to the deputy and see if there are any updates."

"Perfect."

Shane paced through each room. There were no pictures of Verna with the kids in here. No pictures at all, really.

What exactly was Verna like? The photos he'd found online of the woman had never shown her smiling. She didn't have any of her own social media accounts, but she'd shown up in pictures posted by others.

She'd worked as City Treasurer, sending out payment notifications to residents. The job apparently made her unlikable to many since they associated her with bills. But, according to Wilder, she'd done her job zealously, hardly ever letting any delinquent payment slip by.

Madison and her brothers had come to live with Verna after their father went to jail. The oldest brother, Bear, had only stayed a year and a half until he was old enough to move on.

What had life been like for the two left behind?

Shane paused by the room where Madison had been attacked. Based on the pink walls, he guessed this had once been her bedroom.

He studied the door frame and squinted. Marks on the outside indicated that a deadbolt had been there at one time.

The only reason a deadbolt would be on the outside of the door was . . . to trap someone inside.

His gut churned.

Slowly, he opened the door and examined the other side of it.

Scratch marks stretched down the wood. They were old, not fresh. Several marks near the knob indicated someone had tried to pry it open.

His stomach churned harder. Exactly what had gone on inside this house?

He wasn't sure, but he didn't like the picture forming in his mind.

As he examined the room, Brammall's footsteps sounded down the hallway and paused in the doorway. An interruption was the last thing Shane wanted. He hoped his colleague had a good reason for it.

"What now?" Shane gave him a questioning glance.

"Something just popped up online." Brammall's voice caught with anticipation. "You're going to want to see it."

# CHAPTER EIGHT

MADISON RELEASED the breath she held as Isaac's car stopped before hitting anything or running off the road.

Instead, she stared as the figure standing in the road came into focus.

She blanched as she studied the man another moment, suspicion filling her. Finally, she muttered, "Bear?"

He'd changed since Madison had seen him last. Once clean-cut, he now had a shaggy beard. His form had filled out, making him look like a burly linebacker. He wore a flannel shirt, jeans, and work boots.

That wasn't to mention the fact that he held a

shotgun in his hands and a sheathed knife hung from his belt.

Isaac let out a breath and shook his head as if in disbelief also—as well as annoyance. "You've got to be kidding me. What was he thinking? I could have hit him!"

With a glare, Isaac lowered his window and leaned out.

Madison prayed her brother—both of them, actually—kept a level head. The last thing any of them needed was more conflict.

Bear strode to the side of the vehicle and narrowed his gaze as he peered through the window.

"I should have known it was the two of you." His voice contained an edge of hostility.

He was still upset with them, even after all these years, wasn't he? The strange thing was that Madison felt like *she* was the one who should be upset with *him*.

After all, he'd left her and Isaac with Aunt Verna, even though he knew how horrible the woman was.

"You should have told me you were coming," Bear growled.

"Look, can we talk?" Isaac sounded all business. "You know we wouldn't be here unless we needed to be."

His shadowed gaze stared back at them. "Is this about Verna's death? Because I told you I don't care what you do with her remains. I don't plan on going to any funeral or burial or even a tribute."

Isaac and Madison exchanged a glance, unspoken conversations drifting between them.

"No, it's about more than that," Isaac finally said as he turned back to Bear. "I'd feel better if we could talk about this face-to-face."

Bear stared at them another moment, and Madison felt certain her oldest brother would send them back.

Finally, he stepped away and grunted. "My house is just up the road. Keep going until this lane ends. I'll meet you there."

Madison sighed. She hadn't realized just how much tension she would feel when she saw her oldest brother again.

But it was there.

All of it was there. Maybe it had never gone away but had grown instead in the years stretching between them.

How had her family fallen apart like this? Until she was eleven years old, Madison had thought her brothers and father were perfect.

It had just been the four of them. Their mother

had passed away when Madison was only two.

But everything had changed the day her father was arrested.

There was no going back to fix things now.

Isaac continued down the dirt road, his jaw hard as if he dreaded this just as much as she did.

"He has a lot of nerve," Isaac muttered, white knuckles on the steering wheel.

"You know Bear doesn't like to be taken by surprise. He never has. You remember the surprise party we threw for him when he turned sixteen? He stormed out of the house and didn't come back. We all had to party without him."

"Don't defend him."

"He *is* our brother." She shrugged, memories of the party causing a rock to form in her chest. That was one of the last events the four of them enjoyed together before their father was arrested a couple of months later.

"I say he forfeited that when he left us." His scowl deepened.

Madison's stomach squeezed harder. She'd always hoped once her brother turned eighteen, he'd try to claim guardianship of them like he'd promised. But he hadn't. Instead, he'd disappeared, leaving Isaac and Madison to fend for themselves.

He'd known what a horrible woman Verna was. That she was smart. She was able to hide things from the social workers who stopped by for welfare checks.

Isaac, on the other hand, had stayed with Madison until she was old enough to leave. Then he'd helped her apply for grants, secure a job, and set her up in an apartment so she could attend college.

Everything about that time felt so fractured.

As the woods cleared, Isaac pressed on the brakes. A house appeared in the distance.

Madison blinked as she saw it.

She'd expected a shack. With trash and clutter out front. Long grass. Maybe an abandoned car or two.

Instead, the house in front of her looked respectable. More than respectable. It looked *nice*. The outside was a mix of cedar and river rock, topped with solar panels on the roof. The structure rose two stories, with an inviting porch. The flowerbeds contained colorful mums.

At the back of the property, she spotted a detached garage, a small garden, and several chickens.

"What has Bear been doing to afford this?" Isaac

muttered, sharing her disbelief.

"I guess we're going to find out."

They glanced at each other, their look saying more than any words could ever express. They were both apprehensive about this and hoped this meeting went well.

But neither of them really thought that it would.

SHANE'S EYES remained glued to the video playing on his colleague's phone. With each new second that passed, his gut twisted in horror.

The video showed Madison being revived after being found unconscious—unconscious at her attacker's hands.

The lighting was dim, but, just as with Verna, the attacker had worn a camera to record himself bringing Madison back to life.

Shane wanted to look away from the footage, but he couldn't.

He needed to watch, to look for clues.

As the man gave Madison CPR, her eyes suddenly flung open. She gasped in a deep breath, and her chest rose as if her life blood was being restored.

Her relief was short-lived as her gaze went to the camera—or, more accurately, to the man wearing the camera.

Raw fear filled her eyes as she stared at him, and a cry of horror left her lips.

"Please . . . no more. Please!"

Shane looked away as disgust rose in him. "We're going to need to send this to the field office. Maybe our guys in Knoxville can figure out the location from which it was posted. Was it on the same account as the last video?"

Brammall shook his head. "No, it was a new one. This guy is smart enough to know we're monitoring the other one."

"We need to contact the website host and make sure no more of the videos are posted. Can you get on that?"

He nodded. "I'll see what I can do."

As Brammall walked away, Shane glanced out the window. A man lingered near the porch, staring up at Verna's house with open curiosity.

Instantly, Shane reached for his gun.

Who was that man? And why was he trying to peer inside this house?

# CHAPTER NINE

MADISON CLIMBED FROM THE CAR, slammed the door, and turned to face Bear as he slowly walked toward her, clearly in no hurry to catch up.

His cold gaze went to her neck, and he flinched. "What happened to you?"

"That's what I wanted to talk to you about." Madison touched her neck and immediately winced at how sore it felt.

Images of last night flooded her mind, and she felt herself reeling back in time.

*No, you can't go there. Not now.*

She pressed her eyes closed and pulled in a breath. She had to focus on the present, on the good things.

That's what Madison's counselor told her to do

when overwhelming thoughts about her past battered her. *Concentrate on the positive, on the things you're in control of. There's no need to stress over matters that are out of your hands.*

"Did someone hurt you?" Anger singed Bear's voice, and his chest seemed to swell with protectiveness.

*Now* he cared? All those years of being indifferent to her, and Bear suddenly felt protective?

Madison didn't say that aloud, though. This wasn't the time for that discussion.

"Maddie was attacked last night," Isaac announced, his voice matter-of-fact and his shoulders stiff with defensiveness.

"Attacked?" Fire lit in Bear's gaze as he turned back toward her. "Are you okay?"

Madison swallowed back the retorts and tried to restrain her feelings. Nothing good ever came from an emotional reaction.

She didn't always live by that, but right now, she needed to. Emotions were already running too high.

"I'm hanging in." Her voice cracked.

"What happened?" Bear stepped closer.

"Some creep broke into Verna's, strangled Maddie, and brought her back to life—several times." Isaac's lips twisted with disgust as he said the words.

Visible shock rippled over Bear's features. "What … ? Who … ?"

"We don't know," Isaac said. "But the MO matches—"

"Dad's." Bear scowled.

"Matches The Good Samaritan Killer." Isaac raised his chin as if daring his older brother to defy his words.

"Dad's in jail, so you think this is a copycat?" Bear's hands went to his hips as he stared back at Isaac.

"Or maybe Dad was never guilty after all," Madison murmured. "Maybe the real killer has returned."

"We've been through this. We can't live in denial." Bear shook his head. "Our father did horrible, horrible things. We have his blood running through us. And I pray every day that the evil he possessed isn't passed down like some kind of generational curse."

Madison squeezed her eyes shut as her head pounded.

Bear had never believed in their father's innocence.

That was the reason why he'd separated himself from Isaac and Madison.

Lines had been drawn—lines that couldn't be erased. Why were they trying to cross them now? Why rip off this scab? It wouldn't do any good.

"Look, this isn't a time to argue." Madison hardened her voice to let them know she meant business. "We have to figure out what we're going to do."

"We should forget Verna died. You two should go home. And we should pray this ends. Either way, I don't want anything to do with it."

As Bear's words hung in the air, birds squawked overhead.

Madison glanced up and saw three vultures circling them.

Did those birds know something they didn't? Did the creatures know one of them would soon be a goner?

She shook off the thought.

Most likely, a small, dead critter lay somewhere nearby in these woods.

"I'm not sure we're going to be able to forget this happened," Isaac said. "What if Madison is still a target? Otherwise, why wouldn't that guy have killed her last night? Instead, he let her live. Why? Because he wanted to make a point."

"And what would that point be?" Bear's stormy gaze met Isaac's.

Isaac's jaw tightened.

At once, Madison pictured him in the courtroom, passionately arguing his case.

"I think it's clear Dad's not behind this," Isaac said. "That means the real killer has come out of hibernation. I think he's telling us we need to pay for the sins of our father—because when Dad was tried and found guilty, suddenly this guy didn't get any of the attention he fought so hard to achieve."

A cold chill went through Madison.

She wanted to deny Isaac's words. But maybe she shouldn't.

Bear stared at them another moment, his gaze darkening with every passing second. Then he shifted and let out a breath. Still, he remained silent another moment as if coming to terms with something.

Madison knew enough to give him space. He couldn't be pushed.

"There's something that I should show you," Bear finally muttered.

"What's that?" Isaac asked.

Bear reached into his pocket and pulled out a

silver cross dangling from a chain. "I found this hanging from my front door two days ago."

Madison's head began to spin, but Isaac caught her arm before she collapsed.

That cross . . . it was the Good Samaritan's calling card.

He was back, wasn't he?

The serial killer—the real serial killer—had returned again after all these years.

---

"CAN I HELP YOU?" Shane stepped from Verna's house and strode toward the man lingering outside. Shane's hand remained near his gun, just in case. Until he knew what was going on, he couldn't take any chances.

The man was probably in his late fifties with graying hair that had disappeared from the top of his head. He wrung his hands in front of him, looking almost startled at Shane's appearance. "I'm sorry. I didn't come to cause trouble."

Shane flashed his badge and introduced himself.

"I'm Harry Simpkins." The man's voice sounded cautious and maybe even a little weary. "James was my colleague at the school. He was . . . my friend."

Now this guy had Shane's attention. He could be very useful. "What brings you by?"

"I heard Madison had returned for Verna's funeral. I thought I'd stop by to check on her. But then I saw the sheriff . . . and the crime-scene tape. What happened?" He blinked, his gaze almost looked frightened, like he expected the worst.

Shane didn't want word to get out about Madison's attack. He wanted to keep it under wraps for longer if he could. The more time they had without media scrutiny, the better. Dealing with the press on top of dealing with a murder consumed too much energy—and energy was a valuable resource.

"There was an incident here, but everyone is fine."

"That's a relief." Harry's shoulders slumped slightly. "Could I talk to Madison? Is she inside?"

"She's not here right now. But I'd like to ask you a few questions."

"Of course. About what?"

"About James," Shane said. "How well did you know him?"

Emotion flashed through Harry's eyes—a mix of loyalty that waned as doubt battered it. Feelings after events like this were rarely simple.

"Like I said, we were friends," Harry said. "I

hated what happened to him. He would have never killed those women like that. I don't care what anyone says."

His words held more confidence than his gaze, Shane noted.

"Did you keep in touch with the kids after James was arrested?" Shane continued.

"I tried to." Harry's face pulled down in a frown. "But my wife wasn't supportive. She didn't want us to be affiliated with the family. But I hated that they had to come live with Verna."

Shane remembered the evidence that a lock had been on their doors. The scratch marks. The absence of any personal photos and the warmth and welcoming they offered.

"What was so bad about Verna?" Shane wanted to hear this man's perspective so he could form a better picture of this woman.

Harry frowned as he glanced at the house. "The woman was strict. Exacting. I think she resented having the kids at her house. She'd never been married and wasn't exactly a people person. I always worried about them."

"But you didn't try to do anything?" Shane hadn't seen anything in Verna's records about any trouble with police or lawsuits.

"I called children's services a couple of times. But they never did anything. I couldn't help but think that the system had failed them." Harry frowned as he glanced at the road in the distance. "And so did this town, for that matter."

# CHAPTER TEN

MADISON SLIPPED her phone back into her pocket and frowned, the feeling of unrest growing inside her.

Isaac turned toward her as they remained in front of Bear's place. "Who was that?"

"Special Agent Townsend." Madison frowned again as she remembered their conversation.

"Special Agent Townsend?" Bear repeated, emotion suddenly flaring to life in his gaze. "He's still with the bureau?"

"Why wouldn't he be?" Madison had no idea what her brother was talking about. Did he somehow know the man? What sense would that make?

"I figured he would have retired by now. He's got

to be older than fifty-seven—the mandatory retirement age for the FBI."

"I'd guess he's in his mid-thirties," Madison muttered. Her brother wasn't making sense. What had happened in the years since they'd lost touch?

Bear narrowed his eyes. "We must be talking about a different guy. Because the FBI agent who arrested our father was Agent Townsend. But he's older than the man you described."

Madison's mind raced. This wasn't making sense. Unless . . . "Do you think this guy . . . could be . . . his son?"

Isaac shrugged and let out an airy, cynical chuckle. "I have no idea. But the coincidence is uncanny, isn't it?"

Madison let out a breath, liking this Townsend guy less and less. "Yes, it is."

"What did he want?" Isaac repeated, his ever-ready focus present in his gaze.

"He said he wants to talk to me at the station later today when I have the chance."

Isaac's expression darkened. "I can swing you by. First, we need to figure out where you're staying tonight. You can't go back to Verna's."

"Maybe there's room at the motel." He'd

mentioned something about the Whistling Pines on the drive here.

"Probably not at this time of year," Bear said. "Everyone's out here leaf peeping. Everything is booked so I doubt you could get a room."

"My assistant found one for me," Isaac said. "A last-minute cancelation, apparently."

Madison sighed as she realized this might be more complicated than she'd assumed. Her brother probably wouldn't want to share a room. "I'll figure out something."

Bear stared at her a moment, his gaze steady yet uncertain as he said, "You can stay here."

She swallowed hard at that prospect. Staying with Bear would almost seem like staying with a stranger . . . except she and Bear had too much history between them. Staying with him wouldn't allow her any breathing room. Plus, it was so isolated up here . . .

"I couldn't possibly impose—" she started.

"Of course, you can. You're my sister."

"Maybe I'm flesh and blood, but I hardly feel like your sister." She rubbed her throat again. She hadn't meant for the biting words to escape. But they had. Too much emotion had built up over the years.

Bear flinched as if her words hurt. Finally, he

nodded slowly. "I understand. Do whatever you want. But there's room here if you two need it."

Isaac nodded toward his car. "We should get going. We just wanted to tell you what was going on. What are you going to do about the cross?"

"I guess I should tell the sheriff." Bear's words came out flat as if he'd already checked out and withdrawn into his shell.

"You should." Isaac took a step back. "And you don't want anything to do with the graveside service, correct?"

"No, I don't. Verna may have been my blood relative, but she wasn't my aunt." Bear cast Madison a knowing look.

Something about his expression made Madison's lungs feel like they were shriveling.

Coming back here had been a bad idea.

All she wanted to do was leave town.

Maybe she would forget about the graveside service too.

Verna had very few friends. Why did she deserve to be honored? After the way she'd treated Madison and Isaac, no one would blame them if they simply buried the woman and moved on.

So why did Madison feel like she wouldn't be able to live with herself if she did that?

She had some major decisions to make.

BEFORE DRIVING TO THE STATION, Madison and Isaac decided to grab a quick bite to eat since it was well past lunchtime. At first, Madison didn't think she could hold anything down. But now her stomach grumbled, and she knew that she needed to try.

"Bear's a real piece of work, isn't he?" Isaac frowned, not bothering to hide how he felt, as they headed down the winding mountain road.

"He's hard to figure out, that's for sure."

"I just don't understand how he could be so selfish . . ."

"It didn't make sense to me for many years. Finally, I figured I just had to let it go. If Bear doesn't want to associate with me, then so be it. Life is too short to try to force people to be around me."

"I get what you're saying." Isaac scowled. "I just don't like it. I don't like all the memories that being back here is stirring."

Madison forced herself to think about something else. "Let's talk about food instead—it's a much safer subject. There are no fast-food places around here, so where are we going to grab something?"

"How about that diner? Hometown Diner, right?"

She remembered that place. It was right in the heart of Fog Lake. "Do you really want to go out and about in town? What if someone sees us?"

"Maybe no one will recognize us. A lot of the old-timers have probably moved on. It's been almost fifteen years. Don't you think people would have forgotten?"

A ball of ice formed in her gut. "I don't know. Sometimes I don't feel like anyone moves on."

Madison squeezed her eyes shut and remembered all the advice she'd shared with the families she worked with. She always encouraged them to regain their lives. To not live in fear. To keep their heads up.

It only seemed right that Madison should do the same thing. But now that she was back here and facing her demons, the idea terrified her.

"If you want to, I'll run in and order for us. I can bring it back to the car to eat—as long as you promise not to leave crumbs." He flashed a smile.

But Madison knew he was serious. He'd always been a tidy guy.

Madison tried to smile but failed. "That's okay. I can go in."

She might as well get this over with and rip the Band-Aid off, so to speak.

Twenty minutes later, they'd climbed back down the mountain and entered the downtown area of Fog Lake. The thriving tourist town was located on a lake that always seemed to wear a cloak of clouds.

The downtown area stretched beside the water, full of quaint shops around a town square, where concerts were held on weekends. Autumn was show-time for the area, and street corners had been deco-rated with hay bales and pumpkins and other photo opportunities for those visiting.

For most of her formative years, Madison had so many happy memories here. Memories of coming to the fall festival with her family. Of drinking apple cider and entering the pumpkin-carving contest.

But that was all in the past.

She swallowed the lump in her throat. She'd tried so hard to keep her pain locked up and throw away the key. But life had different plans for her.

Isaac found a parking space, and they climbed out, heading down the strip of shops toward the diner.

So far, so good. They had passed a few people, but nobody looked twice at them.

Apparently, word hadn't leaked about what had happened yet. That was a good thing, but Madison knew it was just a matter of time before gossip would spread. People would realize that Verna's death may not have been natural. They'd hear Madison was back in town and had also been attacked. Then rumors would follow about her father.

Leaving right now seemed like the best idea of all. Maybe she could go back to Nashville and pretend that none of this had happened.

But she knew it wouldn't be that easy. This guy hadn't killed her when he had the chance—which could mean he wasn't done with her. If that was true, was there anywhere she'd be safe?

She and Isaac walked into the diner and the hostess sat them at a booth in the corner.

As Madison held up her laminated menu, her hands trembled, giving away her nerves.

"What are you going to get?" She tried to find something normal and mundane to focus on.

"A bun-less burger with a side salad." Isaac closed the menu and set it off to the side, decision made.

She raised an eyebrow. "Watching your figure?"

"Always." He lifted his arm and made a muscle before laughing, not taking himself too seriously.

Madison knew from past conversations that he had to look the part of successful lawyer in order to get the clients he had.

Kate had seemed to fit right into his new lifestyle with her designer clothes and perfect blonde hair.

At the thought of the woman, more questions raced through Madison's head. What was the story between the two?

Madison had met Kate a year ago when she and Isaac had gotten together in Nashville for Thanksgiving. The woman seemed nice enough. But Madison wasn't sure she could see her brother with Kate long-term.

He might give off the impression of a big city lawyer. But deep inside, he was a hometown boy who liked simple things. Most people didn't know that until they really got to know Isaac, away from the job and the rat race.

When her brother was ready—*if* he was ready—he'd fill her in on what had happened between him and Kate.

The waitress came, dropped off some glasses of ice water, and took their orders.

As the woman walked away, Madison's lungs

began to loosen a little bit. Maybe she'd been a little too paranoid about this. Maybe her brother was right, and most people left in town wouldn't recognize her.

As she glanced across the restaurant, she spotted a man sitting alone at one of the booths. He wore all black, including a baseball hat that shadowed his face.

But none of that bothered her. It was the fact he kept glancing at her and Isaac.

Her back went straight.

Had he recognized her?

But that really wasn't what she feared, she realized.

What she really feared was the fact she hadn't seen the face of the person who'd attacked her.

It could be anyone in this restaurant. Madison could be staring right at that person, and she wouldn't even know. Another round of uncontrollable trembles rushed through her.

How was she ever going to get a decent night's sleep again? Because every time she closed her eyes, she began reliving that terrible, terrible night.

# CHAPTER ELEVEN

MADISON MANAGED to force down half of her dinner. Her brother had already eaten his entire bun-less burger and salad. He'd even eyeballed her fries, but, to his credit, he didn't snatch one.

Part of Madison wanted to hurry this meal along. Suddenly, she was anxious to get to the station and find out what Agent Townsend wanted to talk to her about.

Another part of her wanted to put off their meeting as long as possible. Maybe she was better off not knowing whatever it was he had to tell her. What if it was more bad news? Or what if Townsend had found evidence that made her look guilty? He could have the same determination his father had—determination to solve the case, no matter the cost.

"You ready to go?" Isaac nodded at her plate. "Or do you want to eat more?"

"I'm good." Madison stood and started toward the door. Just as she reached it, a man and woman stepped inside.

When Madison saw the woman's face, she drew back.

Liz and Frank Emerson.

Their eighteen-year-old daughter had died at the hands of The Good Samaritan Killer.

"You? How dare you show your face in this town again?" Liz spat out. Her frizzy strawberry-blonde hair sprang away from her face, and her premature wrinkles practically vibrated with every word.

Frank tried to take Liz's elbow and lead her away, but Liz remained rooted in place. Her gaze was fastened on Madison's, untethered rage rising from her.

"Your family only brings trouble. You're not welcome here. Do you hear me? You're not welcome!"

"Liz . . ." Her husband tugged her arm again.

Everyone in the restaurant seemed to go quiet as they watched the scene. Madison felt frozen where she was, unsure what to say or how to react. Thankfully, Isaac took her arm and led her outside away from Liz.

"If you're smart, you'll get out of town and never return again," Liz called through the doorway. "We don't need trouble like you in these parts. We have enough going on without you coming back here to stir up old memories. Do you hear me?"

Even after the restaurant's front door closed cutting off Liz's tirade, the words echoed in Madison's head.

She'd heard her all right.

In fact, the words wouldn't stop replaying in her mind.

SHANE GLANCED AWAY from his chat with Sheriff Wilder as Isaac and Madison stepped into the station.

His breath caught as he observed Madison.

He'd hoped she might look better since he'd seen her last. But, instead, she still looked pale and shaken.

In fact, she almost looked worse, as if she'd seen a ghost.

But he was glad they were here. He'd been

thinking about Isaac and Madison for most of the afternoon. And he had more than one reason he wanted them to come in.

Not only did he have news, but he also wanted to request their help. Those two knew their father better than anyone. Shane wanted to get to the bottom of things, and the siblings could help him find some answers.

If they agreed to do so.

He knew the proposition was risky. But it was worth a shot.

Before they could check in with the receptionist, Shane strode toward them. "Thank you for coming back."

"Of course." Madison nodded almost nervously as she rubbed her hands together in front of her. "What can I do for you?"

"There's something I want to show you."

She licked her lips, clearly still nervous. Her brother touched her back as if trying to calm her.

"Let's go into the conference room."

He led them down the hallway to the room. As the brother and sister sat beside each other, Shane took a seat near them at the front of the table. He grabbed his laptop and found the file he needed.

As the mouse hovered above the Play button, he

hesitated and glanced at Madison. "This isn't going to be easy."

"I don't understand . . ." Madison stared at him as if she hoped his eyes had answers for her. "I'm stronger than you think."

"It's not about being strong. This is about tough things being tough." He drew in a deep breath, trying to find the right words and praying he wouldn't blunder this. "A video popped up online today."

Madison's breath seemed to catch. "What kind of video?"

Even as she asked that question, Shane had the feeling Madison knew exactly what kind of video it was.

"It's a video of you. I thought twice about showing you, but I thought you'd want to know. Maybe seeing what's on this might help us find answers. Besides, I'd hate for you to find out about this from someone else."

Madison shook her head and scooted back in her chair, averting her gaze from the computer. "I don't want to see it."

Shane nodded, completely understanding her stance, yet at the same time wishing she would be willing to watch it for clues. "I'm not going to force you."

"Why would you even think that she would want to see it?" Isaac demanded, something close to accusation in his gaze.

"I was hoping something in it might trigger a memory, might help us figure out who this guy is."

"All I know is that he's not my father. That's the bottom line." Madison crossed her arms, making it clear her opinion was firm.

"We know it's not your father." Shane swallowed hard before adding, "But it could be someone acting as a copycat of your father."

She swung her head back and forth, not even giving his idea a chance. "My father shouldn't be in jail right now. And I know who your father is. He's the one who practically staged a witch hunt in an effort to put my father behind bars. He succeeded. Now you're picking up the torch for him."

Shane sucked in a breath. He'd known it was only a matter of time before Madison put the pieces together. He'd known his bloodline wouldn't work in his favor.

"It's not like that," Shane finally offered.

"I really don't want to be here," Madison spoke up. "Can we go now, Isaac?"

She looked to her brother as if grasping for a lifeline.

Isaac straightened, his gaze suddenly cooler. "Is there anything else you need, Agent *Townsend*?"

"As I said, I'm not going to make Madison watch anything." He directed his gaze to her. "But if there's ever a point you feel ready to, the images could trigger a memory that will help us catch this guy." Shane shifted before he drove home his point. "Honestly, I'm concerned you won't be safe until he is behind bars."

Madison's hand went to her throat again as if she were reliving the nightmare from last night. She quickly shook her head. "No. I can't watch it. Not now."

Shane leaned back, done pushing the issue. He didn't want to invite more trauma into this woman's life. "I understand. But at least let me tell you this. The video is posted online, and it makes it look like this guy is saving your life. A lot of people are applauding this man as a hero."

"That makes me sick to my stomach," Isaac muttered.

"This guy is good at what he does. He makes it look like he's rescuing you, like he's the hero that steps in to save the day. People don't know what he's really doing."

"Can't you trace the IP address or something like they do in all those TV shows?" Madison asked.

"We're looking into it. I assure you that we are. But these things take time."

"I'm not sure how much time I have before this guy might decide to finish what he started with me." Madison glanced down at her hands and squeezed her eyes shut.

Shane could only imagine the inner turmoil she must be feeling. "I don't want to keep you any longer than necessary. But I did have one more question for you both."

She raised her gaze to meet his. "What's that?"

He pulled in a deep breath and prayed he'd say the right words. "I want to go talk to your father tomorrow."

"Okay . . ." Isaac's voice trailed with caution.

"I was hoping that one or both of you might go with me."

He stared at the siblings as he waited for their response.

# CHAPTER TWELVE

SOMETHING close to rage rushed to life inside Madison.

"You want *me* to help *you*?" The derision in her voice almost made her cringe. But there was a time when anger was righteous. This was one of those times.

"I'm not your enemy—" Agent Townsend started to explain.

"You don't get to decide who my enemies are. As far as I'm concerned, all you feds wanted all those years ago was to close another high-profile case and move on, so you zeroed in on my father. You got the wrong guy. The FBI not only ruined my family, but they ruined my childhood and tarnished my future.

And the worst part is: none of them even cared. Why should I expect anything different from you?"

Agent Townsend's eyes widened as if her words surprised him. "I can understand that this might be hard—"

Before Agent Townsend could finish, Madison leaned forward. "I will *not* be helping you. We're not on the same side. Do I make myself clear?"

He stared at her another moment, something glistening in his gaze. Finally, he offered a curt nod. "Understood."

Without waiting for Isaac, Madison stormed from the sheriff's office. It was only when she was outside that she noticed her brother had followed her.

Isaac's hands went to her shoulders as they paused near his car. "Are you okay?"

She started to nod but then shook her head and squeezed the skin between her eyes. "No, I'm not okay. I can't even pretend to be."

"I'm so sorry, Sis." He pulled her into his arms and held her.

But Madison didn't let the tears fall. Too many tears had already been used up. This wasn't a time to mourn. This was a time to act.

She wouldn't help the FBI. But she *did* need to

find answers. Isaac was an excellent lawyer. Certainly, he could help her. Together, maybe they could track down the person who'd killed Verna. Maybe they could put all this behind them. Was that asking too much?

Madison didn't know. Maybe it was.

But the thought of finding answers was the only thing giving her hope right now.

And hope was something Madison desperately wanted to cling to.

***

THE TALK HADN'T GONE the way Shane had planned. Then again, what had he expected? Of course, Madison and Isaac would have hard feelings toward the FBI after what had happened. He couldn't blame them for that.

But Shane needed their help to find the person responsible for what was going on. He didn't want someone else to become a victim. Nor did Shane want this guy coming back to taunt Madison again.

How could he prove to Madison that she could trust him?

"I've got an update for you." Brammall paused in front of him.

Shane shifted in his seat. "Go ahead."

"The medical examiner went back and ran additional tests on Verna Colson's body. Just as you suspected, he found traces of hydrofluoric acid, which—"

"Can cause a heart attack and is nearly untraceable—unless you know what you're looking for," Shane finished. "The product is also readily available. So, this guy stopped her heart, revived her, and then stopped her heart again."

Brammall shrugged. "That's how it appears."

Tension crawled up Shane's spine.

Someone dangerous was out there.

Playing this deadly game.

A game where he looked like a hero when he was actually a killer. A wolf in sheep's clothing. Anything but a Good Samaritan.

This guy was recreating the crime spree Madison's father had begun.

This copycat needed to be put behind bars for a long time.

Even though it might be emotionally difficult, Madison could offer some insight into this. This man had been close enough to put his hands on her. To kill her. Then revive her.

Shane's gut clenched at the thought.

He'd specifically targeted Madison. But why?

At first, Shane wondered if this guy might be an accomplice to the Good Samaritan. But there was one important detail the FBI had never shared with the media.

Whenever the Good Samaritan struck, he'd carved GS on the tender skin on the underside of his victim's arms—close to the armpit where it wasn't always visible.

When Verna's body had been found, no initials were left behind.

Sheriff Wilder stopped by his desk. "I wasn't trying to eavesdrop, but it didn't sound like that went well."

Shane frowned as he remembered the conversation, the accusations, the hurt. "It didn't. Not by any stretch of the imagination."

"The Colsons were such a happy family." Sheriff Wilder sat across from him, almost as if settling in for a talk. "James Colson was respected in the community. All the kids at school loved him. It was such a shock when we found out he was responsible for these murders. I remember hearing my father talk about it. He was sheriff in this town before I was."

Shane's curiosity lit. "Do you know of any other

suspects locals talked about at the time? Some people that might not have made it into the FBI's investigative files?"

Wilder let out a long breath. "Let's see, there was Ed Beasley. He was a drifter who came into town and slept on park benches and begged for money. A lot of the locals thought he was the one behind it because the crimes began shortly after he arrived."

"But?"

"Three years into the murder spree, Ed died of liver failure. The murders continued."

Shane frowned. "Who else?"

"There was another town troublemaker, a guy name Leonard Kincy. He owned a local auto repair shop—if you want to call it a shop even. It was closed most of the time because Leonard couldn't get his act together. He was actually seen with Vivian Lilies, the third victim. He gave her a hard time when she brought her car in for a flat tire. Some people thought he was trying to flirt with her. Others thought he was entirely too aggressive."

Shane remembered seeing Kincy's name in one of the reports, but he hadn't been arrested. "Why did you rule him out?"

"His mom became terminally ill, and he drove down to Georgia to be with her. Stayed a month.

One of the victims died during that time, and he had an iron-clad alibi."

Shane took a mental note of all these details, just in case.

"And the last guy was Ted Russo. He's the head of Parks and Rec in town—"

"Currently?"

"Yes, he still holds the position. He was found on the side of the road, helping a woman who'd been hit by a car. He'd been jogging and wearing a GoPro. When people saw him . . . they assumed the worst."

"But he was also cleared?"

Wilder nodded. "He was. The woman confirmed it wasn't Ted who hit her."

"What about Harry Simpkins?"

"Harry?" Wilder raised his eyebrows. "He's well-liked in town. Seemed to be a good friend to the Colsons. As far as I know, he was never on anyone's radar."

"And last question—what happened leading up to Colson's arrest? What made them so sure he was the murderer—from your perspective?"

"His truck was spotted in one of the videos, and law enforcement suspected it was a misstep on the killer's part—that it had accidentally been left there. Others said he was never the same since his wife's death. He was also a former volunteer paramedic, so he had the know-how to bring these people back to life. Add to that the fact that he was deeply religious, and it seemed like a slam dunk."

"But that's all circumstantial."

Wilder frowned. "The final piece of evidence came from Madison. She told the feds she'd seen her father leave the house at night on more than one occasion—some of which matched the dates of the victims' murders."

Shane's heart pounded harder at the revelation. "Did she want to make him look guilty?"

"That's not what I understood. From what I heard, she was clueless that her statement might harm her father, and she was devastated when she realized it had. She said her father always told her to tell the truth. She just didn't realize the consequences of that truth."

"What was his excuse?"

"He didn't have one."

Shane let that sink in for a moment. Why hadn't James Colson defended himself?

Maybe because he was guilty.

# CHAPTER THIRTEEN

ISAAC GLANCED at his sister as they paused outside the Whistling Pines Motel. The place had been designed to look like an oversized log cabin, and it offered a view of Fog Lake. Overall, the accommodations weren't that bad.

If only he were here to enjoy them.

Madison nibbled on her bottom lip, as she often did when nervous, as she looked up at him. "Are you sure you don't mind if I stay with you? I feel like I'll be in your way."

"I can sleep on the floor. I don't mind. Really."

"No, I'll sleep on the floor. It's no big deal. Or I can keep looking for somewhere else to stay."

He didn't like the mere mention of that idea—not after everything that had happened. "I'm not comfortable with you being alone right now. Not until we know exactly what's going on."

She frowned but nodded. "The truth is, I don't want to be alone either."

They walked up the stairs to the second level and found their room.

She wobbled a moment as if her legs were weak. Isaac caught her elbow before sticking the key into the lock and pushing the door open.

"It's nothing fancy, but it's a warm place to sleep, right?" he offered.

Madison glanced inside the outdated motel room and shrugged. At least it appeared clean. "It will work."

A few minutes later, they were settled into the room, and Madison hopped in the shower.

As she did, Isaac stepped outside to give Madison some privacy, as well as to get some fresh air and clear his thoughts.

He leaned on the wooden railing near his door and tried to compose himself. The view of the misty lake and the surrounding evergreens helped.

Views like this always did.

He didn't want his sister to know how shaken he felt over everything. As her brother, he felt the need to protect her. He always had.

Unlike Bear.

Isaac frowned at the thought of his older brother.

He'd long ago stopped trying to figure Bear out.

But Isaac hadn't given up on his dad. In fact, his dad was the reason he'd become a defense attorney. He wanted to help others whom the justice system had failed.

His father's image passed through his mind—an image of him sitting in jail.

Maybe it would be a good idea if Isaac and Madison went to visit him tomorrow with the FBI agent.

What was that saying? Keep your friends close and your enemies closer?

Maybe Agent Townsend would show his hand and let them know what he was thinking in regard to these crimes. Maybe they could play nice in order to find out information.

He was going to have to think that theory over.

Isaac pulled out his phone and saw he'd missed calls from several clients. Tomorrow, he'd need to call them back. Unfortunately, he was right in the middle of several cases. He knew he wouldn't be able to stay in Fog Lake long, but he didn't want Madison to have to handle Verna's death alone either.

He paused as he scrolled down his screen and frowned.

Kate.

She'd probably called him ten times already.

Isaac had told her where he was going. It wasn't like he'd left without any type of explanation.

But the numerous calls were typical of Kate.

His head pounded harder at the thought. The two of them needed to have another talk. But it would have to wait until he got back from Fog Lake.

A woman stepped outside four doors down, tucking her key into her back pocket. She appeared to be close to his age and had long, dark hair and a bright smile.

She glanced at him and murmured, "Beautiful evening."

"It really is. No better place to be than Fog Lake with this kind of weather in the fall, am I right?"

She paused long enough to send him an approving smile. "Yes, you're definitely right. Maybe we'll run into each other again."

In different circumstances, Isaac might like that. She was stunning, with a beautiful face and curves that could grace the cover of magazines.

But that didn't matter. Not now.

Not with Kate still in his life.

Not with Madison's safety on the line.

Not with Verna's graveside service to plan.

Isaac simply cast the woman a grin before stepping back toward the motel room.

He and Madison still had a lot to talk about.

---

MADISON LEANED BACK IN BED, her thoughts racing. She dreaded the thought of going to sleep. She dreaded it *so* much.

As she hugged the covers against her chest, she stared at Isaac as he lay on the floor and punched the pillow beneath him. They'd chatted for quite a while, and, at moments, it had felt like old times.

Except that Dad was in prison and Bear had practically disowned them.

And someone had tried to kill her last night.

Madison frowned.

"What are you thinking about?" Isaac propped himself up on his elbow and looked at her.

She shrugged. "Everything, nothing, and anything in between."

He sat up. "I had a thought."

"What's that?" Maybe this would be a good

distraction from her other more worrisome contemplations.

"Maybe we should go with Special Agent Townsend to visit Dad tomorrow."

Surprise zinged through her. "Why would we want to help this guy?"

Isaac shrugged. "I don't really see it as helping him. I think we should go in order to find answers."

Madison stared at him another moment, trying not to let her emotions get the best of her. "You actually think Dad has answers?"

"I don't know. But maybe Dad knows something that can help. Maybe someone contacted him. Maybe the real killer has taunted him. We won't know until we talk to him. When was the last time you went to visit?"

"I go every month. You?"

He leaned against the dresser in his undershirt and sweatpants. "It's been a few months now."

Madison gave him a questioning look.

"I mean it when I say work has been really busy," Isaac finally said, a smidgen of guilt creeping into his gaze.

"Then why don't you try to ease up on your workload?"

The look Isaac gave her made it seem like there

was more to the story. How had the two of them lost touch like this? They used to tell each other everything.

Isaac released a long sigh. "I wish I could but . . . as they say, it's complicated. Anyway, I just think we should consider visiting Dad. I want him to hear what's happening from us. He'll also want to see you himself so he can know that you're okay."

Madison frowned. She hadn't thought about that. "I'll consider it. But I don't trust that man."

"Agent Townsend?" Isaac sounded halfway surprised.

"The one and only."

Her brother leaned closer, narrowing his gaze. "Is that because he's a fed? Or because he's working this case?"

"Both—and because of who his father is." Her words left a sick taste in her mouth. Talk about things coming full circle . . . she'd never expected that now.

"Not everyone with a badge is a bad guy." Isaac said the words gently as if he didn't want to stir up trouble—only offer some wisdom.

Madison frowned. She knew that. She really did.

But when she'd needed law enforcement the most, they'd let her down. They'd ruined her life.

Over the years, she'd tried to move past that. But the task had felt nearly impossible.

Before they could talk about it anymore, she flipped off the lamp beside the bed. "Good night, Isaac."

"Night, Sis."

Madison sank down beneath her covers.

But she had a feeling she wouldn't be getting any sleep.

# CHAPTER FOURTEEN

MY HUNGER GREW.

With each passing moment, my cravings increased.

My show with Madison had been satisfying, but those feelings had only been temporary. Like being given a sample of a tasty creation and knowing afterward that you needed to buy a lifetime supply.

I wasn't done with Madison. She had to know that. I'd given her all the hints, almost like a taste test so she could know what was coming next.

Because, even though there were others out there, I had my eyes set on her.

She was the *crème de la crème*, as the French might say.

I sat in the diner now with my cup of coffee in

front of me, and some rubbery eggs and cold, limp bacon on my plate, as Gloria Gaynor sang, "I Will Survive."

As a waitress passed, I smiled. Of course.

Blending in was important.

So was doing research. Knowing your subject matter. Planning your methods.

Around me, I heard people beginning to murmur. What happened was finally starting to catch wind, and now rumors floated in the air, luring people to gossip like a fresh-baked apple pie lures people into a bakery.

Soon, fear would spread.

I smiled.

I liked fear.

More fear would soon take over this town.

I grabbed a piece of bacon and tore into it with my teeth. As the meat ripped apart, I chewed and chewed and chewed. With every bite, more anticipation grew inside me.

# CHAPTER FIFTEEN

"WE WON'T BE able to bury Verna for at least four more days." Isaac gripped the phone in his hand as he turned to Madison the next morning.

Madison paused mid-sip of the tasteless coffee Isaac had retrieved for her from the motel lobby. "Four more days? Why so long?"

He shrugged and lowered himself across from her into one of two seats near the window of the motel room. "The ME needs more time before he releases her body, for starters. I know we decided not to have a formal service for her. Just the graveside, right?"

"That's right." Madison leaned back in her chair, deep in thought. "But I know you have work you need to get back to. Me? I can work wherever. I know that's not the case with you."

Isaac glanced at his phone again and frowned. "Unfortunately, I do have a couple of pressing cases I'm working right now. I knew I could get away for a couple of days. I guess I can do my best to work from here until I can get back."

Before she could talk herself out of it, she grabbed one of the doughnuts Isaac had brought and took a bite of the yeasty glazed treat. It practically melted in her mouth.

She might regret this later, but, for now, she would enjoy this. "What are we going to do for four more days?"

"There's lots of stuff we still need to figure out, like life insurance and contacting social security and figuring out finances and putting the house on the market."

Madison frowned and took another bite of her doughnut. She was fortunate that she'd never had to deal with these issues before. She'd been too young when her mom had died, so she didn't even remember the funeral. This was the first time she'd ever really had to handle all a death involved.

Isaac rose and shoved his phone into his pocket. "Let's go ahead and reserve the earliest slot at the cemetery. If I have a chance today, I'll write up the obituary so we can get that in the paper and let people know about the graveside service."

"Do you think anyone in town will actually come?" Had everyone been able to see through Verna? Or had she covered up who she really was when she was around others?

Isaac shrugged. "I don't know. I really don't know what Verna's life has been like over the past decade. I don't care to know. She did have a few friends back when we were kids. They were all sour-faced, though, just like she was."

"I know."

"I need to make some phone calls. This case I'm working has some pressing matters that can't wait."

"I understand." Madison nibbled on her bottom lip another moment. "Do you think I should call Special Agent Townsend?"

Her brother stared at her before nodding. "I don't think it's a bad idea. Any insight that we have into what the FBI is thinking could ultimately help us."

Madison finally nodded. "Let me give Townsend a call and see if he has left yet for the prison. You can stay here and work. I'll go."

"Are you sure?"

She nodded. "I'm positive."

"Okay. It sounds like a plan."

But Madison would be lying if she didn't admit that she was dreading this whole experience.

---

"YOU CHANGED your mind and want to come?" Shane leaned against the doorway to the conference room and pressed his phone to his ear as he listened to Madison Colson on the other end.

He hadn't expected to get a call from her—not after their last conversation.

"If you're going to talk to my dad, I would like to be there," Madison announced.

His pulse quickened. "Of course."

"Only one condition."

"What's that?" He waited, curious about what she'd say.

"I want to be able to hug my father."

Despite himself, he smiled. "I think I can arrange that. What about your brother? Is Isaac coming also?"

"Unfortunately, he's not going to be able to make it. Is that a problem?"

Shane shook his head. "Not at all. I can swing by to get you in about thirty minutes. Does that give you enough time?"

"That'll be fine." Madison rattled off the address of the motel.

But Shane already knew where it was. He wouldn't be much of an FBI agent if he didn't stay on top of the details.

He also knew about the confrontation yesterday at the diner between Madison, Isaac, and Liz Emerson.

He could only imagine how ugly that scene had been.

He had a feeling things were only going to get uglier in this town before they got any better.

Shane ended the call and began to collect his thoughts. He'd already called the prison to arrange the meeting. It was located in Knoxville, an hour or so drive from here. Knoxville was also where he lived and where the FBI field office was headquartered.

Maybe it would be good that he and Madison had that time to talk. He wanted to get past her walls and find out if she knew anything else. But that would be easier said than done.

Still, he would give it his best effort.

He had a feeling this guy was getting ready to strike again.

That meant no one in this town was safe.

# CHAPTER SIXTEEN

MADISON STARED out the window as she rode down the highway beside Special Agent Townsend.

If circumstances weren't what they were, she might admit that the man was incredibly attractive. His blue eyes were simply mesmerizing. And even his leathery cologne made her want to lean closer for another whiff.

She'd done some research on him before he picked her up. He had graduated from Clemson University with a degree in criminal justice. He appeared to be single. When he let down his guard, he actually looked like he might be fun—at least, that's what she'd gathered from the photos she'd seen on social media.

There had been photos of him windsurfing. Hiking. Skiing.

He seemed like an all-around well-rounded guy.

Even his SUV looked neat—but not in an over-the-top way. An empty water bottle sat in the console, and a stray leaf or two lay on the floorboard. But it somehow smelled like a football inside—leathery and outdoorsy.

If Madison had her way, she wouldn't talk to the man for the entire trip. But she doubted that would be possible.

"How are you feeling today?" Townsend glanced at her.

She reached for her neck again and touched the bruises there. The reaction was pure instinct. Quickly, she dropped her hands back into her lap.

She'd tried to cover her bruises with makeup so her father wouldn't see them. She'd even picked out a shirt that rose higher than normal on her neck. But, if she moved just the right way, the bruises peeked out and shouted their secrets about what had happened to her to anyone looking.

"I've been better." Her voice sounded entirely more melancholy than she would have liked, and even the strands of Dave Matthews' "Where Are You

Going" on the radio couldn't conceal her anxiety. "But I'll get through this. I always do."

"What happened to you was horrible. And I'm sorry. I'm going to catch the person who did this to you. Who attacked your aunt."

Her throat tightened at his words. "You have leads?"

She seriously doubted he'd answer that question, but she asked anyway.

"Not yet. We've studied the videos and collected evidence from your aunt's house. But, so far, we don't have any good leads. However, our investigation is just starting."

"I see." She stared out the window again, not wanting to engage any more than necessary.

As far as she was concerned, this man was her enemy. It didn't matter if he was handsome or smart or if he seemed likable. Those things were only more weapons in his arsenal that he could use to hurt her.

"Do you get to see your father often?"

"I try to make it about once a month. I'd come more often, but it's a long drive from Nashville." Madison glanced at him, deciding to turn the tables. "Where are you from?"

"I grew up in Knoxville, but my father was transferred to DC when I was a teenager."

"Did you request to come back here once you went through the FBI Academy?" She couldn't help but wonder if he had a sick fascination with his father's past cases and that was how he'd ended up working on this exact one.

"Believe it or not, I didn't request to come back to this area. It just worked out that way, which is fine by me. I think the mountains of East Tennessee are some of the most beautiful in the world."

His answer surprised her. Madison had wanted a response she could offer a sharp retort to. But Agent Townsend hadn't given her any ammunition.

Smart man.

"This area is nice," she said. "There's nothing quite like the Smoky Mountains."

"I like it. But it's hard trying to live in your father's shadow—and that's what I feel I'm doing here." His voice sounded sincere, almost regretful.

Was he just trying to get Madison to warm up to him? To trust him so she'd share her secrets?

She wasn't sure.

But she couldn't refute his statement. She knew all about living in her father's shadow.

Townsend glanced at her. "How did you end up in Nashville?"

Relief filled her. Nashville seemed like a safe enough subject—safer than talking about murder, at least. "I started my nonprofit and knew I needed to be centrally located. But I wanted to be close enough that I could visit my father, so Nashville made the most sense. It gave me enough distance from this area that I didn't have to worry about running into people from Fog Lake and seeing the judgment on their faces."

Townsend's lips pulled down in a frown. "I imagine it wasn't easy going through what you did."

"It wasn't." Madison clamped down and stared out the window again. "But I try to use the experience to help others."

"What exactly do you do with Blood and Water?"

"Whenever I hear about a family going through something similar to what I experienced, I contact them and offer my assistance. If they accept, I fly to wherever they're located and sit down with them to find out their needs."

"Where did the name come from?"

"In the Bible, it talks about how blood and water escaped from Jesus' side during his crucifixion. That blood and water represents forgiveness. That idea, combined with the fact that family is our blood, and that water can be cleansing, just made sense to me."

"I like that. And what kind of needs were you talking about specifically when you mentioned helping families?"

"Sometimes, they just need to know that someone else has been through what they have and came out okay on the other side. Other times, they need financial assistance, or they want to relocate, or they're unsure how to move on. Do they cut ties with their loved one in prison? Do they remain loyal? It's a hard place to be."

"I can imagine."

"I've worked with some wonderful people—people connected with cases I'm sure you've heard about. Lenora Anderson's husband killed four prostitutes before being killed by police. Clarissa Daniels' father was discovered to be the head of a drug ring known for killing multiple people. Annette Peters' son was a school shooter. Belinda Cox's brother killed the rest of her family and would have killed her too—except she got home late because of traffic, which ultimately saved her."

"Those are some pretty high-profile cases."

"They are. But there are more victims than the ones who died. There are the victims who just happen to be collateral damage as well. They deserve to be noticed. To be helped. To have hope."

Finally, the Knoxville skyline came into view.

It was almost time to see her dad.

Madison didn't know whether to be excited or to dread this. Or maybe, honestly, the answer was both.

She hated to dredge up bad memories for her father. The last thing she wanted was to make his life harder by adding to his worry. But she also hated seeing that look of despair on his face. Hated seeing what prison had done to him. He'd once been so youthful and vibrant and friendly.

Now, sometimes, he seemed like a shell.

Agent Townsend turned into the lot and parked.

Before they climbed from the SUV, Madison turned toward him. "I don't want my father to know I was attacked."

"Don't you think he'd want to know?"

"I don't want him to worry. He's already been through so much."

Townsend stared at her a moment before nodding. "If that's what you want."

"I do. Thank you."

They climbed out and began walking toward the building in the distance.

As they did, Townsend turned toward her. "Listen, since we're going to be unofficially working together, why don't you call me Shane?"

"That sounds good. You can call me Ms. Colson."

He stared at her a moment as if trying to figure out if she was joking. Then he let out a chuckle.

The moment seemed to break the tension between them . . . for now, at least.

SHANE CAREFULLY WATCHED James Colson's eyes when he saw his daughter walk into the private visiting room.

The man's gaze went from hard to teary-eyed. "Madison . . ."

She crossed the room and threw her arms around him without a moment of hesitation. She clearly didn't fear her father.

Next, the man's gaze turned to Shane. Shane offered a curt nod before flashing his badge. "Special Agent Shane Townsend. Thank you for agreeing to meet."

Something flickered in Colson's gaze. The man had recognized his name. People had always told Shane he looked exactly like his father, so no doubt this man had put the pieces together.

Shane knew that his father's legacy might ultimately harm his chances of getting Colson to say anything. But, still, he had a job to do.

"You look like a chip off the old block," Colson said.

"My father and I might look alike, but that doesn't mean that we are." Shane's voice hardened. It wasn't that he didn't like his father. But he and his father weren't the same man. Their decisions weren't the same decisions. Their paths weren't the same.

Colson continued to study him, a cautious look in his gaze. "Clearly, you followed in his footsteps. So you can't be that different."

Shane understood the man's point, and this wasn't the time when he needed to explain himself too much. His father may have been a good man, but he was also an imperfect man. A workaholic. Narrow-minded. Constantly distracted.

"I heard he passed last year of cancer. I just wanted to tell you I'm sorry."

Colson's words caused a knot to form in Shane's throat. He hadn't expected compassion from the man.

He managed to pull himself together long enough to nod and mutter, "Thank you."

He lowered himself into the metal chair across

the table from Colson, and Madison followed his lead, sitting beside him. But Madison's gaze remained fastened on her father. Occasionally, she tugged up the neckline of her sweater, probably trying to conceal the bruises there.

"What brings you here?" Colson's voice turned no-nonsense, as if he sensed something big had happened. "And what brings you with my daughter?"

Shane swallowed before starting. "I'm not sure if you've heard anything about this yet. But we believe that your sister died at the hands of a copycat killer."

"What?" Colson blinked several times, and his voice sounded wispy with disbelief.

"It initially appeared Verna died of a heart attack," Shane continued. "But a video surfaced that matches the MO of your previous crimes."

Colson's gaze narrowed, and his posture suddenly became more rigid. "Let's be clear about something. If you want my help, then you need to stop referring to what happened as *my* previous crimes. To this day I've maintained my innocence, and I will continue to do that. Are we clear?"

Shane stared at him, at the convicted hardened criminal who'd gotten away with murder seven times before being caught.

If he wanted answers from this man now, Shane needed to play nice. It was only smart.

"We're clear." Shane offered a clipped nod. "Do you know anything that might lead us to finding the person who did this to your sister?"

"How would I know? I'm in this prison, and I don't get to see or talk to anyone except my cellmates. I'm not sure why you thought I might, and, in that case, I'm sorry you wasted your time by driving out here."

Shane sensed he was beginning to lose Colson and knew he needed to change tactics. "We believe this person is somehow connected with your family. Whether or not you're guilty of the crimes you're in prison for, something connects you with this murder. We're trying to figure out what that might be."

Colson shrugged, his posture softening, but only slightly. "I don't know what to say. I hate to think about my sister suffering at the hands of someone imitating the Good Samaritan. But I have no information for you."

"Did you have any of your own theories?" Shane veered into a different approach. "Did you have any suspicions about who this killer was? Because if you're not guilty, someone clearly framed you."

Colson's gaze darkened. "I've thought about it a lot. And I just might have a few theories."

Madison sucked in a breath beside him, as if she hadn't expected her father to say that.

Shane couldn't wait to hear what he had to say. At this point, they needed a break. Would Colson be the one to provide that?

# CHAPTER SEVENTEEN

MADISON LEANED CLOSER as her father began to speak.

"I still think Ted Russo should be considered." Her father's jaw flexed as if he were restraining his emotions and concentrating instead on the cold hard facts.

"The Parks and Rec guy?" Shane clarified. "Why should we consider him?"

"You know he was accused of the crime in the beginning." Dad paused. "Personally, I think he set up that fiasco on purpose."

"Why would he do that?" Madison couldn't figure out the logic behind her father's statement.

"I think Ted wanted to clear himself once and for all—and to toy with law enforcement."

"But the woman said Ted wasn't the one who hit her," Shane reminded him.

"That's true. But she was bleary-eyed with pain," her dad continued. "Plus, I know for a fact that Ted Russo liked nothing more than pretending to be someone else."

Shane shifted. "Would you care to explain that some more?"

Her dad raised his chin. "Of course. Ted was always in charge of the town's Trunk or Treat celebration. Every year, he came dressed up as someone new—Superman, a mime, Dracula. His costumes were stellar. He said his aunt used to work in Hollywood and taught him a few tricks of the trade. He was also skilled at using latex face makeup."

"So, you think he disguised himself first, just to throw the police off his trail?" Shane asked.

Her dad shrugged noncommittally. "It's a theory. I have more."

"Who else?" Shane asked.

"Arnie Siebert."

"The emcee guy?" Madison blurted. Arnie often emceed events in town, acting as host and spokesperson with his showman ways.

Her father nodded. "That's right. He's always had a bitter edge about him when it comes to women. He tries to come across as charming, but one of my students told me he hit on her—and when she rejected his advances, he became angry."

"But that doesn't make him a killer," Shane said.

"I agree. But he likes attention. He was also a news anchor out in Missouri before he was fired for sexual harassment."

"So, he knows how to handle himself with a camera," Madison said.

"Exactly." Her dad's eyes lit with pride. "He told me on more than one occasion that his father was a doctor—"

"And his father could have taught him some healthcare basics," Madison finished.

"Exactly."

Shane's gaze flickered between the two of them. "I'll look into them. Do either of those men have a reason to target you? Because, if you're not guilty, then someone set you up."

Dad remained quiet a moment before letting out a long breath. "The only person I could see targeting me is Arnie. I encouraged my student to tell the police about what he did. He wasn't happy with me afterward. He stormed over to my house and told me off. He's got quite the temper."

Shane nodded slowly and scribbled some more notes. "Thank you. I'll see what I can find out."

Madison reached across the table and squeezed her father's calloused hands. She missed him so much and hated seeing him in this state.

His hair, always thin, was now almost completely gone. He had an oval face and kind eyes. He'd always been on the shorter side, but he'd carried himself like a giant.

Now he looked gaunt but more muscled. He had more wrinkles. A tougher edge to him.

She supposed he had to develop that in order to survive in the prison system.

"What happened to your neck?" He frowned as he nodded at her bruises.

Madison released his hand and pulled her jacket collar up higher. "Nothing."

"It's bruised." Tension stretched taut through his voice. "*Something* happened."

She tried to swallow, but a knot had formed in her throat. She'd wanted to ease her father's worry, not add to it. "It's nothing that you need to worry about. Really."

"It's not that new man that you started dating, is it? Eric?" Fire lit in Dad's gaze.

"Eric and I broke up a few months ago," she

assured him. "And no. He had issues, but he never hurt me."

Realization seemed to dawn across her father's gaze. "*He* did this to you, didn't he? The man who killed Verna?"

Panic began to flutter inside Madison. He wasn't supposed to know that. "Dad . . . it's nothing—"

Her dad's gaze flew to Shane. "You can't let him harm her."

Shane glanced at Madison but remained silent, almost as if he didn't want to confirm her secrets.

But there was no use in hiding what had happened anymore. Her dad knew the truth. His fatherly instincts had kicked in.

"Isaac's in town," she finally rushed. "We're staying together. He's keeping an eye on me. You don't have to worry . . ."

"Isaac's a good brother. So is Bear. I know they'll look after you." His gaze turned back to Shane. "But I need you keep my girl safe also."

"I will." Shane's voice almost made him sound like he believed those words, that he did want to keep her safe.

"Even if I was guilty—and I'm *not*—my daughter doesn't deserve to suffer because of my perceived sins. Just like I don't hold what your father did to me against you, I'm asking you not to hold it against my daughter either." Her dad's gaze burned into Shane.

A lump formed in Madison's throat as she glanced at Shane. She halfway expected the agent to scoff or smirk. But he didn't.

Instead, his gaze locked with her father's. "I won't let anything happen to her. You have my word."

Her father reached up and rubbed at the corners of his eyes as if tears had formed.

"Time's up," a guard announced, stepping into the room.

Before Dad was escorted through the door, he turned back to her. "Did you ever find my papers at Verna's house?"

"Your papers?" Madison had no idea what he was talking about.

"Yes, they were there . . . and with her death . . ." But before he could finish his statement, the guard walked with him into the other room, and the door slammed behind them.

Papers? It must have something to do with Verna's death. Maybe her last will and testament, the one Isaac had mentioned.

Just as happened every time she had to leave her father, tension clawed into Madison's chest and heart.

Life just wasn't fair sometimes.

It was a lesson she apparently needed to keep learning.

SHANE WASN'T sure what was changing inside him. He'd always believed that James Colson was guilty, that the right man was behind bars and a killer was off the streets.

But something about seeing Colson and his daughter interact had planted a smidgen of doubt inside him.

What if this man *wasn't* guilty? The question almost felt like a slap across his face.

He couldn't think like that.

Even serial killers had soft spots. And Madison was clearly this man's soft spot. It was easy to see why. The woman gave Colson something to be proud of. She was beautiful. Successful. Generous. Truly, there was nothing about the woman not to like.

After going through the checkout procedures, Shane placed a hand on Madison's back and escorted her from the prison. Neither of them spoke until they climbed back into his SUV.

Finally, he managed to ask, "You doing okay?"

Madison nodded, even though her gaze looked anything but okay. "I hate seeing my dad like that. You have no idea. He used to be so warm and fun. We'd go fishing together. He'd make me grilled cheese sandwiches and tomato soup. On chilly evenings, we'd sit outside by the bonfire, and he'd tell us stories." Her voice choked. "It's not fair. Even though I know that life isn't fair, that doesn't help me come to terms with the fact that my father's life has been ruined."

Shane gave her another moment before he cranked the engine. "Look, how would you feel about grabbing a bite to eat before we head back? It's lunchtime, and, I don't know about you, but I'm getting hungry."

"Lunch is fine." She didn't sound overly enthusiastic or adamantly against it.

"I know a great barbecue restaurant we can try then." Maybe eating together would help her loosen up some and trust him. Food had a tendency to do that.

But first, he needed to call Brammall and ask him to look into Ted Russo and Arnie Siebert.

# CHAPTER EIGHTEEN

HILLBILLY'S WAS a barbecue restaurant located in a strip mall. When Madison had seen the location, she didn't have high hopes the place would be any good.

But the smoky, spicy scent of pork and ribs surrounded her as soon as she walked inside the place, and she began to change her mind.

She and Shane sat at a corner table, and the waitress took their orders.

Then awkward silence had fallen as she glanced across the table at Shane.

She didn't want to admit it, but the man wasn't as vile as she'd assumed.

She'd learned in life that it was easy to vilify someone, to put them in that box and make them stay there forever. But that wasn't fair. Everyone had character fails in their lives at some point. No one wanted to be defined by those moments.

They chatted about Knoxville until their food came, delivered to them in red baskets with buffalo check paper at the bottom.

Madison lifted up a silent prayer before digging in.

She took a bite of her sandwich, the vinegar from the barbecue mixing with the tangy coleslaw topping it. "This is good."

He smiled. "I told you."

Her gaze locked onto his. "You have no obligation to keep me safe, by the way. I know you told my father that just to make him feel better."

Shane instantly seemed to sober. "I do have an obligation to keep you safe. It's part of my job."

"You really think this guy isn't done yet?" Madison hardly wanted to ask the question, but how could she not? Just what was in store for her future? It wasn't like this was the first time she'd asked that question.

Shane picked up another fry. "It's likely. He could have killed you, but he didn't."

"You think this guy is killing people because of some kind of vendetta against my family?"

"Clearly, your dad is in prison, so we know he's not involved. The fact that you were targeted . . . yes, it does make me think this is out of revenge or that this guy is trying to make a point."

Madison waited a moment before saying, "Some people thought The Good Samaritan Killer had an accomplice. Some of the video angles seemed to indicate someone else was filming, but it could never be proven."

Shane studied her without apology. "I read that in the files also. Let's say that's true. Do you think this accomplice could be the one who attacked you?"

"Not really. I think the guy who attacked me is a copycat."

"What makes you so sure?"

"Instinct."

He nodded slowly before taking a sip of his sweet tea. "What about your father's theories? What do you think?"

Madison let out a deep breath trying to collect her thoughts. "I think they have merit. I think he's had a lot of time to think about things. And I think the real killer is still out there, so why couldn't this guy be Ted or Arnie?"

Shane nodded.

"Are you really going to look into them?"

"Absolutely."

Shane's phone rang, and he glanced at the screen before frowning. "It's my partner. One minute."

He put the phone to his ear and muttered a few things to Brammall, if Madison remembered the man's name correctly.

As Shane pulled the phone away from his ear, a grim expression remained, and Madison knew that something was wrong.

"We've got to get back." He rose from the booth and dropped some cash on the table, the majority of their food already eaten.

"Is everything okay?"

"Another video surfaced."

Her breath caught. "Of whom?"

"Someone new." His gaze met hers. "I'm not going to watch it until I get back to Fog Lake. But we need to get going."

Madison's head spun as he escorted her from the restaurant.

Another person attacked?

She pressed her eyes closed for a brief moment as she lifted a prayer for the victim and any loved ones whose lives would be forever changed.

SHANE'S THOUGHTS continued to race as he headed down the highway back to Fog Lake.

Another victim? It was too early. Too soon.

This didn't match the previous MO.

In fact, this new killer almost seemed manic for another victim.

That didn't bode well with Shane. His muscles felt taut at the thought of it.

He didn't want to watch the video until he was somewhere he could give it his full attention. Plus, he didn't want to watch it either in public or with Madison nearby—not until he knew what he was looking at first.

"You're worried." Madison's voice cut through his thoughts.

"I'd be a terrible FBI agent if I wasn't."

"Do you think if I left this area, Fog Lake would be safer?"

He thought about her question a moment. "Honestly? I think this guy may have lured you here by killing your aunt."

As Madison sucked in a quick breath, Shane instantly regretted his words. But even with the regret, what he'd said was true. Maybe it was better if Madison knew that.

She was inexplicably tied with this killer. How far would he go to make a point?

Shane didn't want to even think about it.

He glanced in his rearview mirror. The same car had been following behind him for the past twenty or so miles.

Had the killer found them?

That didn't fit the Good Samaritan's MO. But this guy wasn't doing things by the book.

Maybe because he wasn't the same guy.

Madison glanced behind her. "What is it?"

"I think we're being followed." Shane turned off the highway, needing to test his theory.

Watching in his rearview mirror, he saw that the other driver followed him.

He clamped his jaw tighter.

As the road became less congested and the car remained behind them, Shane jerked the wheel to the left.

His SUV stopped, blocking the street, and preventing anyone from getting past from either direction.

"Stay here!" he barked to Madison.

He grabbed his gun and jumped from the front seat, ready to confront the person behind them.

# CHAPTER NINETEEN

MADISON COULD HARDLY BREATHE AS she waited to see what would happen next.

Certainly, this guy wasn't brazen enough to follow them now. That wouldn't fit the mental picture she had of this killer.

This copycat operated under the cover of darkness. Under the cover of being a hero.

He didn't chase down FBI agents in broad daylight.

Then again, this wasn't the real Good Samaritan Killer either.

She craned her neck and saw Shane approaching the vehicle, his gun drawn and his stance stiff, defensive.

He appeared strong. Capable. Safe.

*Safe*? Where had that thought come from?

This man wasn't on her side.

But there were very few people in Madison's life she had thought that about. Mainly, her dad. She'd always known everything would be okay when he was close.

Then he'd been taken away.

Would Shane be taken away right now also?

She swallowed back a cry as fear rose in her.

*Please, God. Don't let Shane get hurt. Please.*

Madison might not like the man, but she didn't wish him any harm either.

She watched as a man—slightly overweight with kinky dark curls and glasses—stepped from the dark-green sedan with his hands raised in the air. His gaze darted around nervously, his motions appearing stiff with fear.

Madison's breath released in a quick puff.

A killer wouldn't act like that, right?

Unless he was trying to trick someone.

Her thoughts continued to race. She lowered the window so she could hear their conversation.

"I'm sorry," the man said. "I didn't mean any harm."

"Leave your hands in the air and step away from your vehicle," Shane ordered.

"I'll do whatever you say." He took several steps away from his sedan and toward Shane.

"Who are you?"

"I'm Robert Levada," the man said slowly. "I'm a crime beat reporter from Knoxville. I heard rumors about what's going on in Fog Lake, and I wanted to check it out."

"So, you're following us?" Shane's voice hardened as if he grew more irritated by the moment.

"Please, let me explain. I went to the prison to see if I could talk to Colson. When I got there, I saw Madison Colson and decided to follow her instead. I hoped I might be able to stage a meeting and ask her a few questions."

Shane narrowed his gaze. "You were in the restaurant too, weren't you?"

Robert's eyes widened as if he hadn't expected Shane to notice that detail. "I'm sorry. I don't mean any harm. I don't. I'm just trying to get a feel for what's happening. Has the Good Samaritan returned?"

Shane stared at the man and kept his voice even as he said, "I don't know what you're talking about."

"I beg to differ. If the public is in harm's way, they deserve to know."

Madison continued to hold her breath as she

listened. She could understand both perspectives. Keeping these tragedies quiet kept people calm. But, by not sharing this information, people didn't know to be on guard.

"If the FBI wants to make a statement, we will," Shane finally said. "If you continue following me, I'll arrest you. Do you understand?"

Robert narrowed his gaze but nodded resolutely. "I understand."

"Now, get back in your car and drive away. If I see you following me again, I'll charge you with obstruction of justice."

The reporter scrambled back into his vehicle and, a moment later, pulled away.

Shane stormed back to his SUV and slammed the door, clearly not happy.

But at least a serial killer hadn't been following them.

That was good news . . . right?

SHANE'S THOUGHTS raced for the rest of the ride back to Fog Lake.

He started toward the motel when Madison's

hand clamped his forearm. "Can I go to the station with you?"

"Why would you want to do that?"

"I want to see the new video."

The video. He had no inkling what was on it. "I'm not sure that's a good idea."

"Clearly, it's public anyway. Either you show me, or I'll find it before the site has a chance to take it down."

As he stopped at a red light, Shane turned toward Madison. "Why do you want to see it?"

"I thought you wanted my help, my insight into people who could possibly have a connection with my father."

"I thought you weren't willing to give that help." There was no need to beat around the bush. The two of them needed to be on the same page instead of at each other's throats.

"I wasn't willing to watch the video of me being attacked, that is true." Madison stared at him, her gaze tumultuous—and stubborn. "But I want this guy to be put behind bars more than anything."

"Then we want the same thing. What's been holding you back?"

"You."

He lifted his brows in question.

"Your father put my father away. I don't know if you can be trusted."

He felt the shadow form over his gaze. "You should know better than anyone that the child shouldn't suffer for the sins of the father."

Madison's eyebrows shot up. "You're saying your father was wrong?"

"No, I'm not saying that." He leaned back, quickly checking the light. It was still red.

She crossed her arms as if unsatisfied. "Then we're still on opposite sides."

"You can sleep at night knowing this guy is out there? Because this is about more than just me and you. It's about the safety of the people of this town."

Madison let out a long breath. "No, actually I can't sleep at night. Literally, I can't."

"Then let's work together." His voice rose with passion. "It will benefit us both—and the people in harm's way."

Madison stared at Shane another moment, and he was certain she would say no. Hesitation marred her every feature, and her eyes almost looked glazed.

"You can watch the video with me, but in return, I'd like your full cooperation with everything else as well. No picking and choosing what you're willing to help with."

She hesitated. Then she nodded and seemed to make up her mind. "Okay. I'll do whatever I can to help. But I'm only doing this for my father."

Satisfaction raced through him. "Fine. For your father."

As the light turned green, Shane headed back toward the sheriff's office.

He thought the two of them could help each other.

But he hoped he didn't regret this.

# CHAPTER TWENTY

MADISON FELT as if her throat was tightening as she sat in Shane's temporary "office" with the computer on the table in front of them.

An army of men stood around her—Shane beside her, Brammall behind, and Sheriff Wilder lingering in the doorway.

Her heart thumped out of control at the thought of watching this footage. *You can do this. You can stay calm and in control. Just keep your thoughts focused.*

But panic wanted to bubble up inside her.

"This showed up about two hours ago," Brammall explained as he leaned toward the keyboard. "We've already been in touch with the hosting company about having them take the video down. I also sent the link to our FBI colleagues in Knoxville to see if they could trace the location it was posted from. Based on past cases, I'm not hopeful, but we had to at least try."

"Good work," Shane said. "Now, let's see it."

Madison braced herself for whatever she was about to watch. She prayed for the victim. Prayed that there would be no more victims.

Brammall hit Play, and a grainy video appeared. The opening images showed, from a side angle, a woman hanging from the edge of a cliff. A man wearing something similar to a GoPro let out an exclamation before rushing toward her and peering over the edge.

The woman's wide, terrified eyes looked into the camera. "Please . . . you've got to help me. *Please*."

"I'm not going to let you fall." A gloved hand reached for the woman.

As the scene unfolded, it appeared the woman's jacket was caught on a branch. The man pulled a knife from his waist and cut her free. A few tugs later, he dragged her from the cliff and onto solid ground.

The woman collapsed into his arms, tears streaming down her face.

"I've got you," the man muttered. "I've got you."

Then the video cut—probably right before the

woman's face could morph into terror when she realized what was coming next: a replay of what had just happened, only without the rescue.

The footage already had three thousand views. Just as last time, comments from viewers were all positive, each praising this guy for being so amazing.

Bile churned inside Madison.

This man was anything but amazing.

He was sick and twisted, that's what he was.

She found herself practically sneering at the screen.

"Play it again," Shane demanded, his voice hard with disgust.

Brammall did as Shane said.

This time Madison leaned closer to the screen, studying each frame for any details she'd missed the first time.

Her breath caught when she focused on the knife the man used.

She'd seen that design before.

Madison willed her breathing to remain steady even as everything began to spin around her.

No . . . this couldn't be.

It *couldn't* be.

"Madison?" Shane turned toward her, seeming to

sense her distress. "Is there something you want to tell us?"

She swallowed hard as she tried to figure out what to say.

Last time she'd answered that question, the feds had arrested her father and put him in prison for the rest of his life.

She had to make a decision, she realized, and she had to make it quickly.

***

SHANE STARED at Madison as he waited for her answer. He was sure he'd seen something in her gaze. Some kind of recognition.

"Is there something I want to tell you?" Madison finally muttered. "No . . . I'm just in shock over seeing this. It's . . . jarring."

"Are you sure?" He continued studying her face.

She ran a hand through her hair, pushing her thick brown locks away from her face and revealing guarded eyes. "I think I'm just tired. Watching that video . . . you were right. It's tough to stomach, especially after everything."

Shane still wasn't convinced she was being completely honest.

But what could she have possibly seen in this video?

He needed to study it again—without her nearby.

"Brammall, why don't you take her back to her motel?" Shane said. "I'm going to try to determine the location this video was filmed so we can find this woman. Maybe we're not too late."

"Of course." Brammall stepped toward the door.

Madison glanced at the screen one more time before rising. With one final look of regret, she followed Brammall out the door.

Shane still felt unsettled. But he had no time to dwell on that now.

Right now, he needed to concentrate on this video.

He glanced up at Wilder, his heart pumping harder. "You recognize the woman?"

"I don't."

"What about the cliff?"

Wilder frowned and shook his head. "I'm pretty familiar with the terrain around here, but it was hard to make out any details. Regardless, I'll ask around to some of the park rangers. They might have a better idea."

He stood as if ready to jump into action.

Shane had a few other questions first.

"Hold up a minute." He fast-forwarded the video, stopping at one image—the only thing that made sense as far as another clue. "Look at the knife this guy used. The top half of the blade has an intricate laser cut design embedded in the steel. Have you seen anything like this before?"

Wilder stepped closer and studied the image before twisting his neck uncertainly. "I can't say I have. You're right—it does look unique."

"I'm nearly certain that knife is what startled Madison." Shane stared at it another moment, unrest jostling inside him. "I'll do some research on it."

"While you do that, I'll get busy trying to find a location that matches the video."

Shane nodded. "Keep me posted."

As Wilder walked away, Shane turned back to the screen. What was he missing?

Madison definitely knew something . . . something she didn't want to share.

# CHAPTER TWENTY-ONE

MADISON TRIED to hold herself together as she rode back to Whistling Pines.

How had Shane noticed the shift in her? Was she that obvious?

Apparently, she was.

Brammall, on the other hand, didn't seem to notice anything was wrong. On the short trip to the motel, he chatted about Fog Lake and football and fishing.

As soon as they pulled into the parking lot, Madison quickly stepped from the SUV and waved at him. "I can handle it from here."

"Not so fast." He cut the engine. "Agent Townsend wouldn't be happy with me if I didn't walk you to your room."

She'd been hoping to avoid that. "I'm sure I'll be fine."

Brammall didn't seem to hear her. Instead, he fell into step beside her and walked up the steps to the second floor. Madison paused outside her room, ready to tell him goodbye again. But, first, she grabbed her key, unlocked the door, and cracked it to show him she was safe.

"Thank you again," she rushed.

"Of course." He flashed a satisfied smile. "You have a good evening."

She watched him walk away before stepping into the room and locking the door.

Isaac met her, a knot of concern on his forehead. "What's going on?"

"There's been another victim."

Isaac's eyes widened. "What? I'm sorry to hear that."

"There's more." She leaned back against the door as she tried to collect her thoughts. But there was no easy way to tell him. "In the video, the killer used a knife to free his victim . . ."

"Okay . . ." He shrugged as if he had no idea where she was going with this.

"Isaac, I don't know how to say this, so I'm just

going to get it out. The knife in the video looked like the knife I saw Bear with."

"What?" The word came out breathless.

Madison quickly nodded, her mind still spinning. "I'm sure of it. It had the same markings. The same design."

"You think Bear might be behind this?"

"I don't know. But we need to talk to him before anyone else traces the knife back to him."

SHANE PAUSED beside his SUV when he heard a car pulling into Bear Colson's driveway behind him. He'd come alone to question Bear.

It appeared he had company.

As a black sedan came into view, he stepped toward the vehicle, his hands on his hips as he waited for the driver to emerge. A moment later, two people stepped out.

Just who he'd expected.

Isaac and Madison Colson.

Madison had the decency to look chagrined when she saw him. But instead of averting her gaze or making excuses, she marched up to him, her hands jammed down deep into the front pockets of her jeans.

"I was hoping you wouldn't be here yet," she admitted.

"So much for working together, huh?" Shane didn't bother to soften his words. She'd promised transparency, and now she was keeping secrets. That didn't bode well with him.

"I wanted to talk to my brother first." She lowered her voice. "I didn't want to throw him under the bus. I'd like to think you'd understand that."

"You didn't think we'd do a good job discerning this information? You thought you were the only one who could?"

"It's not like that. Bear deserves the benefit of the doubt. What I don't want is another witch hunt."

Shane stared at her a moment, a million thoughts racing through his head. But would Madison listen to any of them? It seemed like she had her mind made up.

She thought the FBI was going to go after their first viable suspect and not give up until they had an arrest.

Because she thought that's what happened with her father.

Shane had hoped he'd made some headway with

Madison. He thought she'd begun to trust him a little. But this proved otherwise.

As they stared at each other in a silent battle of wills, the front door opened, and Bear stepped out. His gaze darkened as he scanned the commotion outside his house.

"What's going on here?" He strolled down the steps as he addressed everyone.

Shane stepped toward him, keeping his gaze hard. He pulled out his badge and introduced himself. "I need to ask you some questions."

Bear paused, his hands going to his hips. "Questions about what?"

"Would you like to have this conversation out here, or would you like to go inside and sit down?" Shane asked.

"Out here is fine." Bear practically growled as he said the words.

"Very well." Shane reached for his phone and pulled up the photo he'd taken of the knife in the video. "Do you recognize that?"

Bear only glanced at it a moment before nodding. "Yeah, it's one of mine. So?"

"You're saying this knife belongs to you?" Shane repeated to make sure that he understood correctly.

"No, I said it's one of mine, as in, it's one of the ones I made. Why?"

Shane paused as he tried to figure out the missing pieces. "What do you mean it's one of the ones you made?"

"I have an online business." Bear's words came out sharp but slow. "I make custom knives. I sell them all across the country, some of them even internationally. What's the big deal?"

Things clicked in Shane's mind. "How long have you been selling handcrafted knives?"

"Six years."

"How many have you sold?"

Bear let out a long breath before shrugging. "I couldn't tell you the exact number, but I'd say somewhere in the ballpark of three hundred. It's a nice little side business."

Shane tried to figure out how he'd overlooked this information. He'd done research on this man. "I looked into you, and I didn't see anything about this."

"I don't use my last name when I sell knives. I have a shop set up under my first name only. I'm still not understanding what the big deal is here." Bear glanced at each of them as if waiting for an explanation.

"We believe there's been another victim," Shane explained. "The perpetrator used one of your knives in the newest video."

Realization spread through his gaze. "You mean, another victim at the hands of the Good Samaritan?"

Shane nodded. "That's correct."

Bear's shoulders slumped as if things suddenly made more sense. "So, this guy ordered one of my knives and used it for the crime? I can't believe this."

"We need to see a list of all your customers."

"I can get you that. But I'm in the middle of teaching a class right now. I'm an online professor, and I told my students to read for a few minutes while I took care of something. Can this wait thirty minutes until this class is over?"

Shane shook his head. "No. I'm sorry, but time is of the essence right now. This woman still hasn't been found."

Something else flickered through Bear's gaze before he nodded. "Okay. I'll pull up those records. Come on inside."

GUILT FLOODED Madison as she waited outside Bear's house with Isaac.

Maybe she should have told Shane from the start about that knife. But she hadn't been able to bring herself to do it. Not until she had more information.

Now she knew the fragile trust between them was gone, maybe to never return. That would hinder her chances of finding out more information from the FBI.

Then again, maybe it had been a mistake to work with the FBI in the first place.

She glanced at Isaac beside her, but he was typing something on his phone. Whatever his latest case was, it certainly seemed to preoccupy him.

Madison tried not to form any judgments. She

had a lot of work waiting for her also. But she was trying to wait before diving back into those tasks. She only let herself check her emails once a day and only returned the most important ones.

But she'd never been as driven as Isaac. He'd been the one voted most likely to succeed in middle school—before their father's arrest had turned everything upside down.

Then there had been Bear. He'd been a football player. The gentle giant. The quiet but dependable one.

Until all that fell apart.

Now Bear was selling homemade knives on an online shop? And teaching some type of college classes?

Madison knew it had been a long time since they'd spoken—since they'd *really* spoken. But she found it hard to believe she was this out of touch with him now.

She stood in the front yard with the warm autumn sun flooding her skin. The air was still cool, but the warmth of the sun made it bearable. Still, she pulled her flannel shirt up around her neck as she noted the cheerful mums and pumpkins on her brother's porch.

Any other time, she might relish this snapshot of fall.

But not given everything going on.

Madison couldn't leave until she explained herself to Bear. Though she didn't owe him an explanation, she wanted to give him one. The tension between the two of them left her feeling bothered, although she wondered if they would ever have a close relationship again.

"Sorry I seem distracted." Isaac glanced up from his phone and frowned.

"Is everything okay?"

"There's a court date tomorrow, and I can't get it moved. I'm just trying to figure out what to do. I thought my co-council could handle it, but now I'm not so sure."

"If it's causing you this much stress, why don't you just go back?"

He let out a quick puff of air. "And miss the service? I can't do that. Not to mention the fact that I can't leave you here with all of this happening."

"Then go back for the court date and then come back for the funeral."

Isaac locked gazes with her, questions in his eyes. "I don't think that's a good idea."

"I'll be okay." Even as Madison said the words, she wasn't sure that they were true.

Before they could talk anymore, Shane exited the front door of her brother's house and headed toward his SUV. Bear stepped out behind him, and his gaze went to Madison. Was that . . . hurt there? Did he think she'd betrayed him?

She sucked in a deep breath as she tried to figure out how to proceed. She simply needed to get this conversation over with before more ill-will hung between the two of them.

She climbed the porch steps and paused in front of Bear. "I recognized the knife in the video and was coming here to ask you about it. Townsend beat me here. I didn't throw you under the bus."

"You don't have to protect me, Madison." His voice almost sounded like a low growl. Or was that exasperation?

"I didn't know you designed knives."

He shrugged, his gaze still distant and aloof. "I started making them to pass time, and then a few people told me my designs were actually pretty good. On a whim, I decided to put a few up for sale online, and I was surprised at the response I got. They've been a nice little side gig."

Madison nodded slowly, hating how awkward

this conversation felt. But the years between them hadn't been erased. She had questions for him, but she wasn't sure that she was prepared to hear the answers. The truth might very well break her heart.

Bear nodded to Shane, who remained near his car in the distance, looking at his phone. "I hope the FBI is able to catch this guy. But my offer still stands. If you and Isaac need a place to stay, you're welcome here."

Madison tried to formulate exactly what to say, tried to figure out how she truly felt about the situation. Nothing about this was easy or simple.

"Thank you. I'll let you know, okay?"

Bear nodded, looking as if he wanted to say something else, but before he could, Shane stepped back toward them.

"I'll talk to you later." She quickly offered a small wave to Bear before heading back to Isaac. "I think we can go now," she told her brother as she reached his car.

He slid his phone into his pocket, still appearing as if his mind was in another world. "Are you sure?"

"I'm sure."

Isaac paused by the driver's side door and peered at her over the top of the car. "Where did they get the image of that knife anyway?"

"You didn't hear? I thought I told you. It's from a video of the other woman that was abducted."

"Is the video still online?"

"I don't know. I know the feds were trying to get it taken down."

Isaac typed in a few things on his phone and then a few moments later, he held the screen up. "Is it this one?"

Madison winced as she saw the images there. She quickly averted her gaze, not wanting to see that horror again. "That's the one."

He watched it a few moments before sucking in a breath.

"What is it?" Madison braced herself for whatever he was about to say.

"That woman . . . I've seen her before."

Everything went still around Madison. "You have?"

"She was staying at the Whistling Pines. She walked past me last night when I was standing outside our room."

Madison locked her gaze with his. "Are you sure it's the same woman?"

Isaac glanced at the screen again and frowned. "I'm positive. She was . . . unforgettable."

# CHAPTER TWENTY-THREE

SHANE HAD RETURNED with a few more questions for Bear. He looked up from his talk with Bear and saw Madison and Isaac approaching.

He was still irked with the woman for not sharing the information about the knife with him.

Now she was interrupting him as he was questioning Bear.

"Can I help you?" Shane kept his voice crisp.

"I just watched the video," Isaac rushed toward them, his gaze tumultuous and urgent. "I saw that woman."

Now they had Shane's attention. He turned to fully face them. "Where? When?"

"I was standing outside the motel room last night

when she walked past. She's staying there. Or . . . she was." His voice sounded strained.

"Are you certain?"

"It was definitely her. She's not someone I would forget easily. She was absolutely gorgeous."

Shane pulled out his phone as he stepped toward his SUV. "Thank you," he called over his shoulder to Isaac and Madison.

He needed to get to the motel to see what information he could find on the woman. If he got her name, maybe they could locate her cell phone or even her car.

This new information they'd shared didn't mean that all was forgotten about Madison's secret. But at least it was something.

They had to find this guy before he struck again.

Time appeared to be running out.

---

MADISON FOUGHT the despair growing inside her. The last thing she wanted to be was a hypocrite to the people she'd counseled.

But as she stood outside the Whistling Pines Motel, her lungs felt as if they'd been filled with cement. As much as she tried to suck in deep breaths of air, nothing seemed to work.

Isaac stood beside her, his gaze scanning their surroundings as if searching for trouble. Darkness had fallen, and the town's namesake fog rose around them, making the whole area seem eerie.

Madison glanced through the windows into the lobby. Shane stood inside talking to the motel manager. Madison knew she should go into her room and forget all this. But she couldn't.

That woman—the Good Samaritan's newest victim—had been here. Had been close.

Had the killer targeted the woman because of her close proximity to Madison and Isaac? Were these crimes in some way centered on Madison's family?

First Verna. Then Madison. Now someone staying at the same motel?

It seemed like too much of a coincidence.

In fact, the more Madison thought about it, the more it seemed like the person behind this—the copycat—could be someone who'd been impacted by the Good Samaritan's first killings. Maybe this new killer had thought their father was guilty of killing those other people, and now this guy was getting revenge by preying on people close to the Colsons.

Madison continued to turn the theory over in her mind. The idea made sense to her.

Should she bother to share the theory with Shane?

She wasn't sure.

If she were correct, they could narrow down their suspects by examining the Good Samaritan's victims from fifteen years ago. What if one of the victim's loved ones wanted revenge?

Maybe there was some clue at Verna's they'd overlooked.

She cleared her throat and turned toward her brother. "Dad mentioned some papers he left at Verna's. Do you know anything about them?"

He shook his head. "No, I don't. Probably some kind of legal documents."

"That was my thought too. Did you find Verna's will?"

"To my knowledge, she doesn't have one. That means everything will have to go through probate, which will be a pain. But it's not surprising."

Madison's breath caught as she spotted Shane leaving the lobby and heading toward the stairs as if on a mission. He paused outside a motel room four doors down from Madison and Isaac's room, pulled on some gloves, and unlocked the door.

"That was her room," Isaac muttered with the shake of his head. "This all seems surreal."

"Maybe it's not too late. Maybe they'll be able to find her alive."

"Maybe. But if she was targeted because of us . . ." He rubbed his throat as if it were too painful to complete his statement.

Isaac didn't have to finish. Madison knew where he was going. He'd feel terrible. Guilty. Like everything was his fault.

"I wish I were up there right now," Madison murmured, pulling her arms closer around her chest. "I want to see what's in her room. I want to know who she was and why she was targeted and when she was taken. Most of all, I just want her to still be alive. He left me alive . . ."

"He probably only left you alive so you could watch the horror unfold," Isaac said. "It's like he's playing a mental game with you."

An ache filled Madison's chest.

Isaac was right. This was a game. A deadly game.

Madison pressed her eyes shut and prayed that this woman had somehow survived.

# CHAPTER TWENTY-FOUR



SUSAN ROSELAND.

Twenty-seven years old. A teacher. She'd come down from Cincinnati to help with a volleyball tournament in Gatlinburg.

When Shane had stepped inside her motel room, the first thing he'd noticed was the silver cross hanging from the corner of her bathroom mirror.

The Good Samaritan's calling card. His statement. His claim that this murder was his.

Disgust turned in Shane's stomach at the thought.

He carefully moved around Susan's room searching for any other evidence.

Brammall remained with the motel manager as he pulled security footage from last night. Shane hoped they would find a clip from the motel parking lot that might offer information.

Shane had also put in a request for her credit card information. If they could find out where she went last night, maybe a receipt from a restaurant or something, that could also indicate to them when and where she may have been taken.

He paused in the center of the room and glanced around. The fact she'd been staying only a few doors down from Isaac and Madison . . . how did that tie in?

He glanced out the window to see the two of them still standing on the edge of the parking lot, watching and waiting.

He didn't know the depth of Madison's involvement. But something in his gut told him that all this centered around her. If they could find the connection, maybe they could prevent another murder from taking place.

Maybe they could find Susan Roseland in time.

As his phone rang, he checked the screen. It was Wilder.

Shane connected the call.

"We have a body," the sheriff muttered.

Shane grimaced.

They were too late.

MADISON WATCHED as Shane rushed from the motel room just as another sheriff's cruiser pulled into the lot.

The deputy headed upstairs and talked to Shane a few minutes before taking his place outside the door, no doubt guarding it so no one could get in.

"What do you think is going on?" Isaac leaned closer and lowered his voice as they stood in the back of the lot and watched.

"Townsend must have a new lead."

"That's what I thought too. He's not even acknowledging that we're standing here. You really made him mad, it seems."

Madison let out a deep breath, feeling burdened over what had happened. "We had talked about working together. But when I didn't tell him about Bear's knife, that kind of ruined our agreement—and his trust in me."

Isaac squinted as he scrutinized her expression. "For a minute, you thought Bear might be guilty, didn't you?"

The question knocked the air out of her lungs. She thought she'd concealed her doubts, that she'd kept her sense of loyalty at the forefront of her actions. Maybe she hadn't.

"Why would you say that?" she asked.

"Because otherwise you would have shared the information with the FBI. But a small part of you doubted him."

Madison shrugged and glanced away, her warring emotions making her head spin. "I just didn't want Bear accused of something without hearing his explanation first."

Isaac leaned into her, nearly knocking her off her feet in that way he did when he wanted to offer a hug without actually offering a hug. A bro hug was what she'd always called it.

"You're a good woman, Maddie. You've got a soft heart."

She glanced at her brother, her thoughts racing as she reviewed everything. "What about you? Has your heart become hardened after all these cases you've been working?"

His smile dipped. "I don't know if I'd say that. But I definitely feel more jaded. Then again, I guess I started feeling jaded when I was only thirteen and dad was arrested."

Madison wanted to dispute his words, but she

couldn't. She understood because that was her life story as well. But she still strived to be an optimist.

She watched as Shane hopped in his SUV and headed out of the parking lot without so much as glancing their way.

"Let's follow him." Surprise rippled through Madison, even though the words had left her own mouth.

"Really?"

She only had to think about it for a second—time was a luxury she didn't have right now. Since Shane wasn't likely to share information anytime soon, she'd find out for herself.

She nodded. "Yes, I want to know what's going on."

Isaac hesitated a moment before shrugging. "Let's go."

AS MADISON and Isaac headed down the road, her brother did a good job keeping a decent distance behind Shane. But, knowing Shane, the FBI agent was well aware that they were following him.

Madison's stomach roiled harder and faster as they headed out of town and onto more winding, mountainous roads that surrounded the small community.

Finally, twenty minutes later, Shane pulled to the side of the road behind several emergency vehicles. He climbed out and cast Isaac and Madison a dirty look before charging toward the group in the distance.

Madison's head swirled, and she prayed she didn't pass out from anxiety. What was going on here?

"You still want to do this?" Isaac asked.

She nodded, her stomach still churning. "I do."

She climbed out and hesitantly stepped toward the group in the distance.

They were near an overlook, which displayed a stunning view of the mountains on clear days. Right now, darkness surrounded the area, other than the police lights that had been set up. Crime-scene tape was strung in the distance, and the crowd murmured amongst themselves.

She glanced at the people there as she approached. Most were law enforcement, but several weren't.

Were they tourists who just happened to be here when the body was discovered? Rubberneckers?

Her gaze stopped at one person.

Was that . . . ?

It was.

Arnie Siebert.

What was he doing here?

Her blood felt colder as possibilities ran through her mind.

"Maddie?" Isaac asked.

She drew her attention back toward him, but her head was still spinning.

Isaac nodded toward something in the distance. She followed his gaze and saw a body draped in a sheet in the center of a group of officers.

A cry caught deep in her throat. "No . . ."

"Hey . . ." Isaac turned her away from the scene and pulled her into a hug. "That's not the outcome I wanted either."

"I was just hoping that there was still a chance."

"I know. I know. There's nothing we can do here. Maybe the best thing we can do right now is to get you back to the motel. It's been a long day. We could both use some sleep."

She wanted to argue with him. But she knew that there was no use. Shane wasn't going to share any information with her tonight. If at all.

So where did that leave her?

She still had three days before Aunt Verna's

graveside service. Isaac was handling most of the legal aspects of her death. She had too much time to think. To worry.

Maybe it was better to try to keep her mind occupied with something else.

If only that were possible.

# CHAPTER TWENTY-FIVE

AS MADISON RODE AWAY from the scene, all she wanted was for everything to return to the way it had been before Verna died. She was perfectly content with her life in Nashville.

Sure, catching her boyfriend and her best friend kissing had been difficult. But Madison had moved beyond that and instead poured herself even more into her work. She liked spending time following up with families she'd helped. Having lunch together. Seeing what kind of needs they had and trying to provide solutions for them when possible.

People called her dedicated. And she was.

But she also found working easier than being idle and dwelling on her past.

Life with Verna had been hard. After her dad's

arrest, going to school had been difficult. The kids had accepted them, but their classmates' parents had forbidden most of them from socializing with any of the Colsons. That had made for many lonely days.

Finally, a woman at church named Anita had taken mercy on them. She taught at a Christian school in the town of Pigeon Forge and had offered to drive them there each day. The school had given them grants so they could attend.

Anita's kindness had made Madison's life a little more bearable. One person could indeed change a life. Anita had been part of Madison's inspiration for starting Blood and Water. Several years ago, Anita had moved to Florida. But Madison still tried to stay in touch whenever she could.

"How about we stop by Verna's?" Isaac asked. "The authorities should be done searching for clues in the house by now. We need to look for that paperwork Dad told you he left there. Honestly, I've been putting off the legal aspects of her death for too long."

Madison hesitated to return—for more than one reason. Not only was the place full of bad memories from her childhood, but then there was her attack after returning to town . . .

She shuddered.

Isaac seemed to read her mind. "It's okay if you don't want to go. I understand. But someone's going to have to go eventually."

"Why not now?" she finally said.

Isaac was right. They couldn't delay this forever, especially since they weren't going to be in town much longer.

The closer they got to Verna's house, the more Madison's heart thrummed in her ears. Finally, they pulled up to the clapboard bungalow. Dread filled her until she almost couldn't breathe.

Images pummeled her thoughts. Images of waking up to find that man in her bedroom. Of him climbing atop her. Strangling her. Of losing her life. Of regaining it. Of—

"You don't have to do this," Isaac said.

"Let's just get it done."

They climbed out and walked toward the house. She wanted to squeeze her eyes shut. Wanted to forget all this.

But as long as Isaac was with her, she'd be okay.

Madison swallowed hard as he stuck his key into the lock and opened the door.

The crime-scene tape had been removed. When

they stepped inside, everything looked surprisingly normal.

In these rooms, at least.

"Where should we start?" Isaac turned toward her.

"Aunt Verna's bedroom, I guess. Everything else was always so neat and organized. I can't imagine where else she might have left any paperwork except in her desk."

"Let's start there then."

They moved down the hallway, Madison staying close to her brother.

As she passed her bedroom—the door was closed—more memories haunted her. Memories of waking up in terror. Of hearing the man's voice beside her. Of knowing more pain and suffering was coming.

"What do you think?" Isaac's voice broke her from her thoughts.

"About what?"

"I think we should sell this place and give the money to charity. Maybe your charity."

"I think that's a great idea."

He examined her a moment before nodding. "Good. I was hoping you would." He glanced at Verna's bedroom door. "Let's get this over with."

They stepped inside, and Isaac flicked on the lights.

Her neat-as-a-pen room showcased a lavender flowered bedspread on a metal-framed bed. A glossy antique dresser and nightstand. A mahogany desk in the corner with a white slip-cover chair.

All in pristine condition.

Isaac sat in the chair and opened the first drawer. But before they could begin truly looking, his phone rang. He glanced at the screen and frowned.

"What's going on?" Madison knew there was more to all his phone calls, and she was tired of waiting on him to share details.

He frowned. "I'm representing a record producer in Memphis who was accused of killing his brother. It's pretty high profile, and tensions are running high. A lot of people think he's guilty."

"But you don't?"

He clicked the phone off, not taking the call. "I don't. The whole case is circumstantial. I think some people just want to see a rich guy put behind bars to make a statement."

"Sounds tense," Madison said.

"It is. Anyway, my client—Hazy D. Whitaker—wants me to use his private jet to fly back tomorrow morning for the hearing and then he'll fly me back here."

"You should do it." Madison shrugged, trying to assure him it wouldn't be a big deal. She opened a drawer and shuffled through some lotions there.

Isaac swung his head back and forth. "I don't want to leave you alone."

Madison nibbled on her lower lip. She didn't want to keep Isaac from his job. But she didn't want him to worry about her either.

Then an idea came to her. "I won't be alone. I'll tag along with Agent Townsend."

Isaac cast her a skeptical look. "Really? Does he know about this?"

Madison shrugged. "Even if he says no, I'm sure I can find somewhere to stay safe while you're gone, even if that means locking myself in the motel room until you get back."

Isaac said nothing for a few minutes before asking, "You really wouldn't mind?"

"Not at all." She could tell that this was weighing on him.

"But if something happened to you while I was gone . . ."

"Don't think like that."

"You're a good sister, Maddie." He nudged her shoulder with his fist.

"And you can be a pretty good brother when you want to be." It was an understatement. The only reason Madison was remotely successful was because of Isaac and the way he'd helped and supported her.

With that settled, they turned back to the desk.

It was time to dive in.

"LET'S talk through everything we know," Shane said as he paced the front of the conference table at the sheriff's office.

A new team from the FBI had come in to work with park rangers and examine the scene where Susan Roseland was found. He'd come back with Brammall and Wilder to discuss the case and spell out all the details. They had to find this guy, and they didn't have any more time to waste.

"We have three new victims—Verna, Madison, and Susan. Based on video evidence, it appears all three were victimized by the same man."

"And Madison is the only one who survived," Brammall added.

"Yes, she is. She was left alive, most likely, for a very specific purpose." Shane turned toward his colleague. "Brammall, did you follow up on Ted Russo?"

Brammall straightened. "I did. As you all know, he works for Parks and Rec here in Fog Lake, just as he has for the past twenty-two years. He was suspected originally because he was spotted wearing a GoPro while helping a woman on the side of the road."

"And?"

"I looked into his whereabouts last night. He was on an overnight camping trip with the Explorer Cadets when Susan was attacked."

"It sounds like we can rule him out." Shane rubbed his jaw as he fought disappointment. "I got the footage back from the motel, and I was hoping for a lead there. But someone painted the camera lenses."

"So, there's nothing usable?" Wilder pressed his lips together in a frown.

Shane shook his head. "Nothing. What about the family and friends of previous victims? Do any of them have a criminal record?"

Brammall let out a breath. "I couldn't find anything. I looked into each of them. Of course, family is easy to look into. Friends not so much. But I'm still searching to see if there's anyone I've missed."

"Of course, we still have the knife that Bear made that was featured in the video," Wilder reminded them. "And there was that reporter that followed you."

"I checked his schedule, and he's been mostly working in Knoxville," Shane said. "He appears to be driven to get a good story, but there's nothing indicating he's driven to kill."

"There are always the videos themselves," Brammall offered. "Maybe our guys will be able to find a clue in one of them."

"We can hope." Shane leaned back against the wall, his thoughts racing. "So where does this leave us?"

Wilder frowned. "That's a good question."

TWO HOURS LATER, Madison and Isaac returned to the motel empty-handed.

They'd found nothing at Aunt Verna's place—only bad memories and useless documents.

As they walked back to the motel room, Madison

glanced at the door to Susan's room. Another pang of remorse rose in her.

That woman had been innocent, and now her family and friends would have to deal with the aftermath of her death. It wasn't fair. Life so often wasn't, but knowing that fact didn't make it any easier.

Maybe Madison could at least get some sleep now. Hopefully, the morning would bring fresh perspective.

Isaac unlocked the door, and they stepped inside.

But as Madison reached for the door to close it, a movement across the room caught her eye.

A silver cross dangled from the ceiling fan's blades as they spun in slow circles overhead.

She tried to suppress the scream that rose inside her, but she couldn't.

The killer had been here.

In her room.

What other surprises had he left?

# CHAPTER TWENTY-SIX

SHANE CLOSED the door to Isaac and Madison's room and headed down to the motel lobby where he'd left them.

Madison rose to her feet as soon as he stepped into the room, and her hopeful eyes met his. "Anything?"

He shook his head, wishing he had a different answer to give. "No, I'm sorry. The cross was the only thing of note we found."

She frowned as if disappointed. "How did he get in?"

"Based on the marks on the door, he picked the lock."

Her face paled before she quietly said, "I don't like the sound of that."

"Believe me, I don't either. This guy was clearly trying to send a specific message to you."

She rubbed the sides of her arms as if chilled. "So, what do we do now? I'm assuming we can't go back into that room."

"No, we'll need to preserve it a while longer, just in case."

"That's what we thought," Isaac said. "We've been calling other motels and rental agencies in the area. There's nothing available."

Shane rubbed his jaw. They *could* stay at Verna's house—it had been cleared. But they probably wouldn't want to do that. His impression was that the Colsons still owned their father's house. But he also doubted they'd want to stay there, otherwise they'd already be there.

Madison turned to Isaac, a determined expression on her face. "Let's stay at Bear's."

"What?" Isaac's voice sounded incredulous. "That sounds like a terrible idea."

"He's mentioned that we're welcome. Plus, when you're gone, I won't be alone. Bear can look after me."

That statement caught and held Shane's attention. He tensed as he waited for Isaac's answer.

Isaac didn't say anything for several seconds

before he slowly nodded. "If that's what you want to do, I'll make it work. But that's not my favorite idea. However, we don't have much of a choice at this point."

Shane cleared his throat and stepped forward. "I can escort you back to your room to get your belongings."

Isaac's phone rang, and he frowned as he glanced at the screen. "I'm sorry, but I've got to take this."

"I'll grab your things for you," Madison said.

"Thanks, Maddie . . ." Isaac put the phone to his ear and answered enthusiastically as he paced away.

As he did, Shane and Madison walked quietly beside each other up the stairs. "If you don't mind me asking, where's Isaac going?"

"He's flying back to Memphis tomorrow to deal with a legal issue with one of his cases. He'll come back in the evening."

Shane relaxed a little. At least, she wouldn't be alone with Bear very long. But he still didn't like this. "Must be a pressing case."

"It sounds like it's a high-profile one, from what he's told me."

Shane didn't have to think long before deciding what he should do. "How about if I pick you up tomorrow morning? We can do some digging. See what we can come up with."

She did a double take at him. "You'd do that? Even after I didn't tell you about the knife?"

He didn't think she'd appreciate his reason for offering, so he shrugged and said, "I still think you're a valuable resource."

Her eyes dimmed and she quickly nodded. "Right. I understand. I'd be happy to help with whatever I can."

Shane noted her disappointment at his answer. What was that about? He couldn't think too much on it now. Madison agreed, and that's what mattered at the moment.

"Then it's a plan," he finally said.

They reached her room, and he let her inside.

Several minutes later, after he'd watched Madison pack up their things and drive away with Isaac, he went to his SUV.

As he did, he paused.

A silver cross hung from the door handle.

As Shane's back muscles tightened, he glanced around, wondering if the person who'd left it was still nearby.

He needed to follow up about the security cameras.

Now.

———

BEAR'S EYES widened when he opened the door and saw Madison and Isaac standing there.

"We need a place to crash tonight." Hesitation tainted Isaac's words. "Does your offer still stand?"

"Of course." Bear opened the door wider. "Come on in."

Madison stepped inside the house, surprised by how homey the place felt with its neat leather furniture and modest decorations.

"I have two spare bedrooms upstairs," Bear said. "I'll show you to them."

"That sounds great," Isaac said. "And, if you don't mind, I think Madison and I are both tired enough to go straight to bed. Don't feel like you have to act as host."

His shoulder jerked up in a quick, nonchalant shrug. "Etiquette isn't my specialty anyway, so I think I can handle that."

They followed him up the stairs, and Bear showed them to their rooms.

Madison felt rude, but another part of her was glad Isaac had insisted they were tired. There had already been so much drama. She couldn't handle any more right now.

Instead, she murmured good night, shut the door, and turned to observe her temporary room. White walls greeted her, along with a mission-style bed with a blue quilt and coordinating furniture.

Not bad for her recluse brother.

Madison lowered herself onto the edge of her bed and tried to collect her thoughts.

As she did, Shane's image appeared in her mind.

She had such mixed feelings about the man. On one hand, he almost seemed like a handsome knight who'd ridden into town to save the day. On the other hand, the man's father had put her own father behind bars.

Was Shane prone to jumping to conclusions just like his father?

Was it even fair that Madison was asking herself that question?

Probably not.

The situation between them just felt so complicated.

Her phone buzzed, and she glanced at the screen, halfway hoping it would be Shane with an update.

Instead, it was one of the women she'd worked with through Blood and Water—Belinda Cox.

Normally, Madison would answer. But this time, she texted her assistant instead and asked her to contact Belinda. Madison would touch base in the morning after she'd gotten some rest.

Maybe focusing on other people's problems would be a good distraction from her own issues.

# CHAPTER TWENTY-SEVEN

AS THE SAYING WENT, this wasn't my first rodeo.

My experience went well beyond this week and expanded far beyond this town.

But the theme remained the same.

I had power over people's lives, and I loved that.

Many thought they could sleep again after Colson's arrest so many years ago. They thought that peace had returned to their lives. That evil had been contained inside prison walls.

It hadn't.

I was here now, and they were waking up to that fear again.

I'd watched Madison Colson today. I watched as she left with the fed to go to the prison. I saw them go into Hillbilly's.

I saw everything.

But they never saw me.

I smiled at the thought.

Part of the fun was having the upper hand. Of knowing things others didn't.

I was right there, yet they had no clue.

That fact made me feel powerful. Wonderfully powerful.

As I lingered in the woods and watched the lights glow from the window of Bear Colson's house, I wondered what kind of conversations were going on inside. They were tense, if I had to guess.

I would love to be in there listening. But I couldn't risk that. Not yet.

I had other plans, and I couldn't do anything that might jeopardize my goal.

I would make Madison Colson pay.

I would make law enforcement pay.

And nothing was going to stop me.

# CHAPTER TWENTY-EIGHT

BEFORE ISAAC LEFT the next morning, the doorbell rang.

Madison felt warmth spread through her when she came downstairs and saw Shane standing inside.

"Sorry I'm early," he started. "Busy day."

"No problem." Madison glanced at Bear, who glared at Shane from his spot near the doorway. "I need to go."

"I made breakfast."

The scent of bacon and eggs had filled the house —and was tempting. "Can I reheat it later?"

His gaze flickered as if he didn't like that response. Maybe Bear had hoped they could mend fences over breakfast.

Madison liked that idea also, but she knew she

couldn't keep Shane waiting, especially given the urgency of the case.

"Of course," Bear finally muttered.

"Thanks again for letting me stay here. Tell Isaac I hope he has a good flight, and that I'll see him later."

Bear's gaze remained dark. "Will do."

Before they could make any more awkward small talk, Madison stepped outside with Shane.

The man was dressed casually today in his jeans, boots, long-sleeved shirt, and a dark blue vest that made him appear ready to go hiking.

In the meantime, she'd worn her favorite jeans and another flannel shirt. Fall attire was some of her favorite.

"Are you sure you don't want to grab something to eat first?" he asked.

"I'm sure."

"All right then, let's go."

As she climbed in his SUV, the scent of soap and minty shampoo tantalized her. She quickly averted her thoughts.

She hoped today would be the day they found answers. Speaking of which . . .

"Any updates?"

Shane frowned and shook his head. "Unfortunately, no."

She leaned back in her seat. "That's too bad."

"We were hoping for more answers also."

As he said the words, Madison glanced at him and noticed the slight circles beneath his eyes. Had he gotten any sleep last night?

She would guess no.

This case was haunting him just as much as it was haunting her, wasn't it?

As they neared the town, Shane veered onto a side road.

Madison's breath caught as a moment of fear flashed through her.

What if Shane wasn't trustworthy? What if he had something to do with these crimes? What if—

Her fingers dug into the seat.

*Stop overreacting, Madison. Get a grip.*

Her voice still trembled as she asked, "Where are we going?"

Shane cast a side glance at her. "Have you ever shot a gun before?"

"A gun? No. Why?"

"Because it's something you should know how to do, and I'm going to teach you."

Madison blinked, uncertain if she'd heard him correctly. "Why would you do that?"

"This guy has you in his sights. You need to be able to protect yourself if someone else isn't around to do it for you. I can't let him take you by surprise again."

The concern in his voice surprised her. It wasn't that Madison thought Shane wanted her to be harmed. But she certainly didn't think he cared. Right now, he almost sounded like he did.

"I'm surprised you don't need to work the case. Do you even have time for this?"

"I'm making time." His set jaw made his intentions clear. "I thought the two of us could talk as I teach you. We can kill two birds with one stone, so to speak."

Satisfied he wasn't out to harm her, she settled back in her seat. "So where are we going?"

"One of the guys at the sheriff's office has property out here with a firing range on it. He said I could use it."

Madison hugged her arms across her chest and didn't say anything. Part of her liked the idea of learning to shoot. Of being able to protect herself. Or at least not being afraid of guns.

Her father had never kept any guns in the house. He'd said they were too dangerous.

Yet people thought he was a serial killer.

Maybe that was because people usually saw only what they wanted to.

<hr>

TEN MINUTES LATER, Madison and Shane pulled up to a piece of secluded property on the other side of town.

Nothing else was out here. No houses or buildings.

The colorful trees surrounding the mountainous stretch of land around them were breathtaking. Reds, oranges, yellows . . . each tree seemed to have been painted by an artist. *The* Artist. The fog that settled in low-lying areas added atmosphere to the already beautiful scene.

Shane climbed out and opened the back of his SUV. Madison scrambled behind him, noting that the air was cooler out there. She pulled her jacket closer, wishing she'd brought a scarf. An autumn scent hung in the air—dried leaves, brittle grass, musky-sweet decay.

She joined Shane, watching as he pulled two guns from a black bag.

The next several minutes were spent with the basics of gun safety.

Then Shane placed a hand on Madison's back and led her toward hay bales set up like a table in the distance. Beyond that, she saw targets rose from mounds in the dirt.

Madison wanted to deny the fact that Shane's touch sent heat racing through her skin. But she'd be lying. She was all too aware of his fingers touching her lower back as he showed her how to line up the target in her sights. All too aware of his leathery scent and his startling blue eyes.

She didn't even realize she was holding her breath until Shane lowered his hand. Finally, some of the tension in her lungs loosened, and she tried to steady her breathing.

The reaction was unnecessary. Madison wasn't looking for romance. Even if she were, she wouldn't be looking for romance with someone like Shane Townsend, a man whose father had put her father in prison.

Wouldn't that make for some interesting Thanksgiving family conversations?

She nearly chuckled out loud at the thought.

"Okay, stand with your feet shoulder-width apart and your shoulders relaxed," Shane started. "Always use two hands when you're firing a handgun..."

Shane stood entirely too close as he continued showing Madison the mechanics. He didn't step away until it was time for her to shoot. But, first, he placed some noise-canceling earmuffs over her head and then another pair over his own.

"Keeping your sight alignment, slowly pull the trigger back," he directed.

She swallowed hard before curling her finger toward her. A moment later, the gun blasted. The kickback wasn't as bad as she'd thought it would be.

But her bullet didn't come close to hitting that target.

"It's a good start," Shane assured her, his voice sounding distant through the earmuffs. He fired off a few rounds of his own gun and hit the bullseye each time. Three shots. Three hits.

She glanced over at him. "You do this a lot?"

He shrugged. "It's good stress relief."

Madison fired a couple more times before asking, "Don't you miss your life back in Knoxville? It has to be hard traveling to work on cases like this."

She had to admit she was curious about the man

and wanted to know what he was like without his FBI jacket on.

"I guess I miss parts of it. But I don't have anything holding me there, you know? Not really."

Did that mean no family or girlfriend? Madison had already noticed he didn't wear a ring.

"I feel like you know a lot about me—like my entire life has been under the microscope." Madison decided to get to the point. "But I know almost nothing about you."

"What do you want to know? I'm pretty boring, truthfully."

She doubted that. "How long have you lived there?"

"Five years."

"What do you do in your spare time?"

"I like to hike and ski. I used to play some intra-mural sports—soccer mostly. But I had to cut that out because of my schedule."

"You ever been married?"

"Almost, but no. Olivia—that's her name—had some trust issues after another bad relationship, and she couldn't seem to get over them. Me being out of town all the time only added to those issues. Finally, we decided it was better if we weren't together."

"How long ago was that?"

"About two years. What about you? I heard your dad mention some guy named Eric?"

Madison frowned at the sound of his name. "He and my best friend are now together."

Shane met her gaze, his expression softening. "That had to hurt—losing both at one time."

"It did. But it's better to discover that side of him now rather than after we were married, right?"

"Absolutely."

Several rounds of ammunition later, she finally managed to hit the bullseye.

"Not bad," Shane stepped back and nodded. "You picked up on that pretty fast. But how comfortable do you feel holding that gun?"

She glanced at it and shrugged. "I don't know. Considering the fact my dad hated guns, it's a little weird."

"He hated guns?" Shane narrowed his eyes as if surprised.

Madison cleared her throat, trying to keep any bitterness out of her voice but failing. "I know what you're thinking. How could my dad kill all those women yet say guns are dangerous? I have an answer for you. He could say that because he didn't kill those women."

Shane took a step closer. "Look, I can only

imagine how you might feel being around me because of my father's role in your father's arrest. But I think it's safe to say both of us are simply trying to do our best in our given circumstances, yes?"

Madison nibbled on her lip as she tried to form her response. "So, do you still think my father is guilty based on what's happened this week? Based on how you feel after meeting him face-to-face?"

She held her breath as she waited for his answer. She didn't want to admit it, but Shane's opinion was starting to matter, and not just because he was an FBI agent.

# CHAPTER TWENTY-NINE

SHANE STEPPED BACK and ran a hand through his hair, wishing Madison hadn't asked him his opinion. "That's a complicated question. I want to believe in the justice system. I want to believe our system works."

Her wide, imploring eyes met his. "You can believe that while still acknowledging that our justice system isn't always perfect."

He offered a quick nod, her words clearly full of wisdom. "You're correct. But the evidence against your father . . . it was pretty incriminating."

Madison scowled. "That's because he was set up."

Shane removed his earmuffs, and she did the same.

He softened his voice. "Listen, I don't want to get into an argument with you—especially not when you have a gun in your hands. That wasn't my point in bringing you here."

Madison let out a heavy breath, looking as if she appreciated the olive branch he offered. "I know. I don't want to sound ungrateful. You've been . . . you've been kind to me. And I'm really sorry I didn't tell you about the knife. I just wanted to hear for myself what Bear had to say first."

Shane stared at her another moment, trying to judge the sincerity in her voice.

Finally, he broke from his trance-like gaze and stepped back. The last thing he wanted was to let his emotions get involved in this. That would only lead to trouble.

"We should get going," he said instead. "I need to get back to the sheriff's office and follow up on our newest victim."

When she tried to hand the gun back to him, he shook his head.

"What?"

"You can't carry it on you without a permit. But you can keep it near your bedside at night. I want you to have something to protect yourself with if you need to."

She snapped her gaze away and rubbed her throat as if remembering the danger she was still facing. "Of course."

The bruises on her neck were fading a little. But the reminder was still there. She'd been attacked, and Shane needed to make sure it didn't happen again.

Part of him would love nothing more than to forget about this case and spend more time out here getting to know Madison. But that wasn't a luxury he had right now—not when people's lives were on the line.

SHANE PARKED at the sheriff's office. But, instead of going inside, he and Madison walked down the street to The Busy Bean, a coffeehouse that also sold baked goods.

Sheriff Wilder had been generous and accommodating, and Shane wanted to repay the department by bringing in some treats.

He bought a dozen donuts and then grabbed some gourmet popcorn to enjoy himself.

As they headed back, he opened the bag and offered some to Madison.

"Caramel and cheddar popcorn?" She turned up her nose. "No thank you."

"Don't hate on it until you try it."

She cast him another skeptical glance. "That combination doesn't sound appealing at all."

He popped a couple of pieces in his mouth. "But it is good."

With one more look, she took a piece from the bag.

"You have to take two. One caramel and one cheddar to eat at the same time."

"You're really serious about this."

"You might as well have the whole experience."

She chuckled. "Fine."

She grabbed another piece and popped them both in her mouth. Shane watched as she chewed slowly. A moment later, she nodded.

"I have to admit—I was wrong. This combination of sweet and salty is pretty amazing."

He grinned, feeling unusually satisfied. "See, I told you."

He held out the bag, and she took some more popcorn.

As they strolled along beside each other, Shane glanced around the town of Fog Lake. It was a great place, especially at this time of the year when pumpkins, bales of hay, and corn stalks decorated various corners and storefronts. Families filled the sidewalks, meandering in and out of shops.

This place seemed like the ideal town to raise a family.

If only it didn't have such a sordid history.

Shane's gaze went to a man wearing a black jacket with a black hat pulled low.

Something about the man's shifting gaze caught his attention.

Was this guy watching them?

Shane braced himself for action.

The next instant, a car revved its engine.

He looked over in time to see a little boy dart into the street and into the path of a car.

"Look out," Madison shouted and lunged toward the child.

# CHAPTER THIRTY

BEFORE SHANE COULD GET to the boy, Madison grabbed the child.

She pulled him onto the sidewalk just as the car zoomed past.

With the wind from the car still fresh on his cheeks, Shane tried to see the license plate, but the plate was obscured by a dark tint.

He rushed to Madison as she knelt toward the boy.

"Are you okay?" Madison asked.

The boy nodded, his eyes still dazed with shock.

Knowing that both of them were safe, Shane glanced around again, looking for the man in black.

But he was gone.

Shane frowned. Was that man significant? He couldn't be sure.

The next instant, a woman ran from a candle shop beside them toward the boy.

"Alex! Are you—" The woman stopped midsentence and glared at Madison. "*You* . . . what are you doing near my grandson? Get away from him. I don't ever want to see you talking to him again."

Madison raised her hands and took a step back. "Liz . . . I was just trying to help. I saw the car coming, and then I saw him run into the street, and—"

Liz stormed closer, her face only inches from Madison's. "Do not ever go near him again. You and your kind . . . you're evil."

"Listen." Shane couldn't keep his mouth shut any longer. "This woman just saved your grandson's life. You should be thanking her."

Liz turned her glare onto Shane, looking him up and down as if he were a piece of trash just because he was associated with Madison. "I don't know who you are, but you should mind your own business. And I'd stay away from her if I were you. Her family is bad luck."

Without saying anything else, the woman

grabbed her grandson's hand and hurried back into the store.

When Shane glanced at Madison, he saw the grim lines on her face. He'd known it had to have been difficult to come back here. But maybe he hadn't realized the extent of it.

"I'm sorry you have to deal with that." At once, he had a fresh perspective on what Madison had gone through. The hate. The resentment. The air of being unwelcome.

"Everybody deals with grief in different ways," she said as they began strolling again, her tone more somber now.

He'd expected her to be angry or upset. Instead, Madison seemed resigned to what had happened.

"You're right," Shane finally said. "People do deal with grief in different ways."

Madison shoved her hands into the pockets of her jeans. "Take my family, for example. Bear blames my dad for all that's happened to us. Isaac throws himself into his work in order to forget his pain."

"And you?"

Madison frowned and looked in the distance for a moment. "I suppose I overcompensate by trying to help other people."

"You're doing good work."

Surprise flooded her gaze as if his words had taken her off guard. "Thank you."

He stared at her a moment, nearly unable to break his gaze.

Madison Colson was nothing like he'd first assumed. She was a remarkable woman. There was no doubt about that.

He'd suspected that she had a special grace about her. But now, seeing her act loving to someone who was so hateful toward her? It only confirmed his conclusions.

Shane realized he was staring and looked away, nodding toward the sheriff's office instead. "We should probably get back."

He hadn't meant to spend so much time before returning to work, but he was glad he did.

Madison nodded quickly, her cheeks flushing as she pushed a lock of hair behind her ear. "We probably should."

AS SOON AS they walked into the sheriff's office, Brammall pointed at the TV in the distance. "The media have caught wind of what's going on."

Madison's gaze went to the screen, and she

frowned when she saw a reporter recounting the sensational news story about The Good Samaritan Killer. With each new detail that was shared, Madison's stomach churned tighter. This had been the last thing she wanted.

"Come on." Shane took her elbow and led her into the conference room. "You don't need to see any more of that."

"Reporters are going to start coming after me soon, aren't they?" Madison had her phone set to receive calls only from numbers in her contacts. But that wouldn't stop reporters from hunting her down, looking for an interview.

"Yes, they probably are," Shane said.

She took a sip of her pumpkin-flavored coffee as she debated how she should handle them. "Should I talk to them?"

He shut the conference room door before turning toward her. "I can't mandate what you do. But I'd ask that, if you do decide to talk, that you let us know beforehand. You've been privy to information that the public isn't aware of, and we don't want anything to leak that will give this guy the upper hand."

"Makes sense." Madison sat down at the table across from Shane, unsure exactly what they were going to be doing today. She only prayed they'd find a lead and finally track down the person who was responsible.

Sheriff Wilder knocked at the door before stepping inside. "We think we have a lead on that knife."

Her stomach gurgled as acid filled it.

Madison wanted to think this had nothing to do with her brother.

So why did a smidgen of doubt remain in her mind?

She held her breath as she waited to hear what the sheriff had to say.

# CHAPTER THIRTY-ONE

SHANE FELT a rush of adrenaline at the possibility of a lead.

Wilder glanced at his notes. "A man named Jarvis Duffy bought the knife for his cousin, a man named Cap Duffy who lives in Kentucky. When I asked about Cap's whereabouts, Jarvis told me his cousin is on vacation in . . . where else? Fog Lake."

Shane's eyebrows shot up. "Good work."

"He's staying at the Whistling Pines."

Shane rose from his seat and grabbed his jacket. "Let's go question him."

Madison rushed to her feet. "Can I come?"

Shane stared at her before shaking his head. "I'm not sure that's a good idea."

"I have to agree with him," Sheriff Wilder added. "Especially until we know more details."

"What if I just wait in the car then? I want to see this guy. Maybe I'll recognize him."

The two men exchanged a glance, and the sheriff waited for Shane to make the call.

Shane didn't want to leave her alone, so having her wait in the car might be the best option.

Madison seemed levelheaded enough that she wouldn't try anything risky. At least, Shane hoped that was the case.

He gave her a nod. "Sure. Let's go."

BACK AT THE Whistling Pines Motel, Shane, Sheriff Wilder, and Brammall readied themselves to question this man. Sheriff Wilder had already gotten the key to the man's room. But they were going to try to play nice first, especially since the evidence was all circumstantial.

Shane confirmed Madison was still sitting in the back of his SUV before knocking and announcing himself. "FBI. We have some questions for you, Cap."

He waited, anxious to see if this guy would answer.

There was nothing.

Shane had already checked Cap's information, and he knew the man's run-down Toyota Corolla was parked outside. He should be here.

Shane knocked again, more urgently this time.

There was still no answer.

With a nod at the sheriff, he gripped his gun with one hand and used the key with the other. He then threw the door open.

Just as he did, a man stepped from the bathroom, a towel tied around his waist.

Cap.

The man practically jumped back into the bathroom as his hands clutched his heart. "What's going on here?"

Shane flashed his badge. "I'm FBI Special Agent Townsend. We have some questions for you."

Cap glanced down at the towel at his waist. "Can I at least get dressed first? I won't try anything."

"Of course."

Shane had observed the outside of the motel and knew no windows led to the bathrooms. Cap shouldn't be a flight risk. But they still had to be careful.

A few minutes later, the man emerged, his dark, thick hair still wet and his pale skin seemingly whiter than before. He now wore jeans and a T-shirt that hugged his pudgy midsection.

He sat on the edge of the bed and looked at them. "What's going on here?"

"We have some questions about a knife that your cousin Jarvis bought for you." Shane showed him a picture of the knife on his phone.

Cap glanced at it before nodding. "Yeah, my cousin gave me a knife like that."

That was easier than he'd anticipated. "Do you have it with you?"

"I do. I put all my stuff in that drawer." He pointed to the dresser and started to stand to grab it, but Shane raised a hand to stop him.

"Allow me." He slipped a glove on and opened the drawer. A laptop, a camera, and a couple of T-shirts stared back at him.

But no knife.

"It's not in here," Shane said after checking under the clothes.

Cap's eyes widened. "It should be in there."

Shane checked the rest of the drawers, moving everything aside to make sure nothing had been missed.

It hadn't.

He turned back toward Cap. "When was the last time you saw the knife?"

"I . . . I don't know. I haven't even thought about it."

"When did you arrive in town?"

He counted with his fingers. "Three days ago."

"Three days ago?" That was when Madison had also arrived. But Verna had died before that.

"What's going on here?" Cap's hooded gaze latched onto Shane's.

"We're going to need to take you into the station to ask you a few questions."

His eyes widened with concern. "Is that really necessary?"

Shane nodded. "Yes, it is."

# CHAPTER THIRTY-TWO

MADISON PACED OUTSIDE the interrogation room, the speaker above her on as she watched Shane question this Cap guy.

Shane had said he wanted Madison there to see if she could identify his voice or anything else about him. She hadn't so far, but a cold chill flooded her throughout this whole process.

Sheriff Wilder stood beside her. Madison had only heard good things about the sheriff. In fact, she'd gone to school with his youngest brother, Jaxon, and she'd always thought highly of the family.

"Anything?" The sheriff glanced at her.

Madison turned back to the interrogation, shook

her head, and frowned. "I keep listening, hoping something will hit me. But I'd be lying if I said it did. I feel like I'd know the killer's voice if I heard it again. I can't say with certainty it's this guy."

Shane had spelled out what had happened inside the motel room and had given her an update on the knife when he'd asked her to watch the interrogation.

"Do you think somebody stole the knife and used it for the crime?" Madison asked. "That seems like it would take a lot of planning. I mean, how did this killer know someone with that knife would be in town right now? It doesn't make sense."

Sheriff Wilder frowned and rubbed his chin. "You're right. It doesn't make sense. It all seems too coincidental."

Her thoughts continued to race. "Did my brother make more than one knife that looks like that?"

"My understanding is that each knife is unique but similar. It was hard to get a definitive visual on the actual knife used in the crime because of the grainy quality of the video."

She crossed her arms and sighed. "So, someone else could have ordered a knife that looks similar to the one Cap has and used it instead?"

The sheriff frowned again. "Yes, that's a possibility. We have to examine each clue to see where it leads."

Madison rubbed her arms, unable to shake her chill. "I understand. It just seems like whoever is behind these crimes is working awfully hard to pull my family into this mess."

Sheriff Wilder nodded slowly. "I agree. That knife was definitely used on purpose. Someone wanted to point suspicion at Bear. Most likely, the killer didn't even know this Cap guy would be in town. His presence here was all a coincidence."

"If it is, then you're wasting time with this guy when you could be tracking down the real killer."

Wilder stared back into the interrogation room. "That's correct. The unglamorous side of police work. We follow paths not knowing where they'll lead. Sometimes it's to answers and sometimes not."

"I understand." Her voice sounded thin as she said the words.

Just then, Sheriff Wilder's phone rang, and he put it to his ear. A few minutes later, he turned toward Madison.

"That was Cap's brother," he told her. "He just went to Cap's house in Ohio. The knife is still there. He didn't actually bring it with him."

"What?"

"He made it sound like his brother is absent-minded. Maybe this was all for nothing."

She frowned.

All Madison could think about was how another day had passed and they were still no closer to finding any answers.

---

SHANE DECIDED to have dinner delivered to the station rather than risk facing the media gathered outside.

Thirty minutes later, he and Madison had a spread of street tacos, chips, and salsa in front of them.

"Do you have any more leads?" Madison picked up a crunchy tortilla chip as she addressed Shane.

"We're chasing down everything we can. Clearly, the knife is a great lead, but it also could have been a purposeful misdirect by the killer."

Madison frowned at the thought of how cunning this guy was. "My brother said he's sold hundreds of them. How do you even narrow your suspect list?"

Shane shrugged, almost looking like more of a colleague than an uptight fed. He was letting down his guard some, wasn't he? The thought secretly thrilled her.

"That's a good question." He scooped some salsa onto his chip. "We started by only looking at people nearby who'd bought them."

"For all we know, the person who purchased it could have been out of town and come here just to execute his reign of terror."

"Maybe." He frowned.

"You're convinced this is a copycat?"

"I am." His compassion-filled gaze met hers. "I know that may not be what you want to hear. I know that if it was the real killer coming back to do his deeds then your father would be cleared. I'm sorry I can't offer you that assurance. But I don't believe this guy is The Good Samaritan Killer."

Madison glanced at her food and plucked a piece of chicken from her taco as she processed his words. "I understand. I prefer the truth to platitudes, so thank you."

"We're going to keep looking at all our suspects. We have some of the FBI's best examining these videos. We're doing everything we can to find this guy."

"I just hope he's found before someone else is

harmed." She shivered at the thought of it. Too much had been lost already. Entirely too much.

"So do I." Shane frowned. "So do I."

# CHAPTER THIRTY-THREE

MADISON GLANCED AT THE DARK, winding road as Shane drove toward Bear's house a few hours later.

"Your brother sure seems to like seclusion," Shane muttered.

"That's how it appears."

"Does he do anything that gets him out of the house?"

"I wouldn't know. We lost touch." Madison tried to choose her words carefully.

She wanted to trust Shane, but she wasn't a hundred percent sure she could. The last thing she wanted was for the man to use her words to form a case against her brother.

Shane cast a look at her before his gaze went

back to the road. "Do you mind if I ask why the two of you lost touch?"

Memories flooded back to her, and Madison wrapped her arms over her chest. "Bear is the oldest of the three of us, and, as soon as he was able, he left Verna's house. He didn't try to stay and protect us. He never came to visit or check on us. He was just gone."

Her voice cracked with grief. She'd known Bear's decision had affected her. Maybe she hadn't realized just how much.

"I'm sorry to hear that." Shane's voice dipped with compassion. "Was that surprising?"

"Actually, it was. He was always the protective older brother. He had said he didn't want us to stay with Verna. In fact, he told me when he turned eighteen, he'd fight to get legal guardianship over us. But, instead, he just walked away." Her throat burned as bitterness rose in her.

Madison thought she'd gotten over it, but the memories still hurt even all these years later.

"I can't imagine what that would have been like." Shane slowed as he rounded a bend in the road.

"Isaac and I bonded a lot as a result—that was something good that came out of this. But Bear knew what Verna was like, and he clearly didn't care."

Dark trees surrounded them on their drive, blurring past as they climbed up the mountain.

Shane stole another glance at her. "What *was* Verna like? What was it like living with her?"

Memories began to pummel her, memories Madison would prefer not to deal with. If only that were an option. But being back here in Fog Lake . . . they were hard to avoid.

"Verna wasn't a saint, that's for sure. She never married and never had kids. It wasn't clear to me whether that was by her own choice or just because she never met a guy who could put up with her. But she seemed to resent our presence."

"I'm sorry to hear that." His cheek flickered as if he fought a frown.

"At the same time, I think she was receiving money for each of us from the state, which helped her out with her own expenses. But she was very strict. She made it clear that if we were going to live in her house that we had to abide by her rules."

"That's probably not unusual."

Madison let out another sigh. "In most cases. But Verna's rules were precise and demanding. No lying on the couch. If we wore open-toed shoes or flip-flops, we had to wash our feet before coming inside. We all took turns cooking and cleaning, and everything had to be Verna's standards. If we did something she disapproved of, she would lock us in our rooms, sometimes for hours at a time."

"That explains the marks on the door. I figured they were from some kind of deadbolt. I'm surprised that there were no social service checks on you."

"There *were* a few. But Verna always managed to pull herself together beforehand. It was kind of amazing, to be honest. Now that I'm older, I wonder if she used her position with the city to get a heads-up before the 'surprise' visits."

She glanced at Bear's house as it appeared at the end of the lane. They'd arrived, and she was halfway disappointed. Even though they'd broached some difficult subjects, Shane had been a good listener.

"It seems like you've turned out okay despite all that," he said.

"I'd like to think so," Madison said as Shane parked in the driveway. "But it was in no part due to my oldest brother." Madison let out a sigh and then opened her door. "Thank you for bringing me back here. I really appreciate it."

"I'd feel better if I walked you up just to make sure that everything's good."

She nodded, too exhausted to argue.

Madison felt surprisingly comfortable with Shane as he walked with her toward the door. Funny how at one time this man had seemed like an enemy, but now he almost seemed like he could be a friend.

No, not a friend. There was too much history between them for that to ever be the case. But maybe he wasn't an exact replica of his father.

Just like she wasn't a clone of her father.

---

"I MADE SOME MUFFINS, if you'd like one." Bear nodded toward the kitchen island where a plate was stacked high with the treats.

Madison paused near the stairway. "I'm pretty full right now from dinner, but maybe later."

She hated how awkward things felt between the two of them. But staying here for a couple of nights couldn't erase all the years between them either.

She had so many questions for her brother. But she wasn't sure if the answers would make her feel better or worse.

What if Bear confirmed everything she'd assumed?

What if she asked him why he'd disappeared,

and he told her it was because he didn't care? Or what if it was something else horrible?

Maybe it was better if Madison got through this time and then returned to her life back in Nashville.

Except she knew she couldn't do that until this killer was behind bars.

"Any updates on the knife?" Bear stepped closer.

Madison guessed that was a safe enough subject. After all, Bear already knew about the knife. That information wasn't confidential.

Except . . . what if Bear had made an exact replica of the knife from the crime scene? What if he hadn't told the sheriff and he'd kept the weapon for himself instead?

Her throat tightened. *No, don't think like that, Madison. Your brother doesn't have anything to do with these crimes. You're being ridiculous.*

"The police thought they had a lead, but it turned out to be nothing," she finally said. "They're still tracking down people who've ordered knives that looked similar to the one in that video."

Bear crossed his burly arms over his chest, his gaze tumultuous. "I hate to think that the killer is using something I created to commit these crimes. Makes me sick to my stomach."

His words sounded sincere, his tone disgusted.

He wasn't faking that, right?

The fact that she even had to ask herself made unease flutter inside.

Madison glanced at her watch. Isaac should be arriving back within the next hour.

He'd be a nice buffer for this conversation.

In the meantime, she nodded toward the stairs. "If you don't mind, I'm going to take a quick shower. It's been a long day, and I need to unwind."

"Of course. Extra towels are in the cabinet over the toilet."

Madison hurried upstairs and turned on the water. Before she started to undress, she realized she'd forgotten her shampoo. She must have left it at the motel.

Certainly, Bear had some extra. She'd seen some boxes in the closet in her room.

Quickly, she hurried across the hall and opened the closet door. Madison began browsing through the items stored there. Extra towels, shower curtain hangers, a hair dryer.

She frowned.

A zippered bag at the back of the shelf caught her eye.

Shampoo? She doubted it. But she'd check just to be sure.

Madison set the bag on the bed and unzipped it.

Her eyes widened at what she saw inside.

Silver crosses.

*Uncountable* silver crosses.

A knot formed in her chest.

Why in the world would her brother have these?

Unless he really did have something to do with these murders.

As the thought slammed into her, Madison glanced up.

A shadow filled the doorway.

It was Bear, and his eyes gleamed with an unreadable emotion.

# CHAPTER THIRTY-FOUR

"THAT'S NOT what it looks like," Bear started, his words sounding slow and purposeful.

Madison stepped back as fear clutched her. "Is there something you need to tell me?"

"I'm not a killer."

Trembles overtook her body as reality continued to hit her. What if her brother was behind all this and she'd just been making excuses for him?

"That's not what all the evidence is adding up to look like." She glanced around, looking for something to defend herself with. Looking for a way to escape.

But there was nothing. She was trapped in this bedroom.

Her lungs tightened at the thought.

Bear turned his pleading gaze on her again. "Madison . . . you know I'm not a killer."

"I'm not really sure I know you at all anymore."

"Can we go into the living room—somewhere a little more comfortable—and talk? I can explain this."

He sounded so convincing. But someone had tried to kill her.

And it couldn't have been her brother. Surely, she would have recognized his voice . . . right?

"I think we should call Agent Townsend." Her voice quivered with fear.

"You don't want to do that." Bear's voice sounded as tense as his eyes looked.

Was that a threat? Madison wasn't sure.

"Madison . . . you know me." Bear's voice remained calm. "I think you know the truth."

The truth seemed murky right now. "I don't know anything right at this moment. I don't want to be here. I just want to go."

He raised his hands as if making a peace offering. "I'm not keeping you here. But I wish you'd let me explain."

"No . . . not now."

Bear stepped back. "I'm not trapping you here, Madison. You know I wouldn't do that."

She stared at him another moment, trying to gauge the sincerity in his voice.

Could she really make it past him? Or was this just some type of trap? Would he grab her if she tried to run?

Fear continued to rush through her until she could hardly breathe. She had to make a decision, and she had to make it quickly.

As he stepped back farther, she inched closer to the door—to her escape—her gaze never leaving him. She couldn't turn her back on him. Not yet.

Slowly, she edged through the doorway, just waiting for Bear to lunge at her.

But he remained where he was.

When she reached the hallway, she continued backing down it.

But as soon as she reached the stairway, she broke out in a run.

She stumbled and fell as she hit the last two steps.

An ache pulsed through her knees at the impact.

With shaky hands, she pushed herself up and darted toward the door.

Just as she opened it, another figure filled the space.

She swallowed a scream and stumbled back, feeling as if she were caught in a snare.

---

ISAAC'S EYES hardened when he saw the terror on his sister's face.

"Madison?" He quickly glanced around, looking for any signs of danger. What was going on here? Had that man come back?

She scrambled to her feet and ran to him. "We need to get out of here."

"What's happening?"

"I can explain later. We don't have time now."

He glanced up again as he saw Bear slowly walking down the steps, a somber expression on his face. Missing pieces clicked in place.

"Did you do something?" Isaac demanded.

His brother raised his hands and shook his head. "No, I didn't. I told Madison she could leave if she wished to."

Isaac glanced at his sister, knowing there was more to this story.

He knew Madison wanted to get out of here, but the analytical side of him needed more information.

Had his brother done something?

"He has crosses," Madison rushed, panic cracking her voice. "Lots of crosses. Like the ones left at the crime scenes."

Isaac pushed Madison behind him as alarm raced through him. He glared at Bear, daring him to lie. "Is that true?"

"She didn't give me a chance to explain."

"Explain what?" Madison asked, her voice trembling. "How you're the actual serial killer?"

Bear reached ground level, paused, and crossed his arms. "I'm not a killer. I ordered those crosses because I'm trying to figure out who was working with dad."

"What are you talking about?" Isaac asked.

"I've been ordering crosses from sites across the country trying to find one that matches the ones left at these crime scenes. That's why I have those. Not because I'm the one behind this."

"Why do you think there's an accomplice?" Madison asked.

"It's a hunch. I never saw these crosses delivered to our house, and I was usually the one who got the mail. That meant someone else must have ordered them. It's been my goal over the past several years to figure out who this other person is."

Madison grabbed Isaac's arm and held tight. "Can you prove they were ordered for research?"

"None of the crosses matched the one from the crime scenes exactly. But, Madison, you would have known if that man who attacked you was me. Right?" Bear stared at her as if trying to see the truth in her gaze.

Madison's grip on Isaac's arm seemed to loosen. "I don't know. I don't know anything anymore."

"You guys really don't think I'm the one behind this. Do you?"

Isaac stared at him another moment.

"I think we should hear him out," Isaac told Madison. "But we won't if you don't want to."

Madison said nothing for a moment until finally releasing his arm. "I'll listen. But I'm going to call Townsend at the first sign of trouble, do you understand?"

Bear's eyes glinted. Was that with admiration?

Isaac wasn't sure.

But he had to give props to his sister. She sounded tough right now.

"Okay, five minutes."

# CHAPTER THIRTY-FIVE

A FEW MINUTES LATER, they all sat in the living room, Isaac and Madison beside each other on the couch and Bear across the room.

Madison still wasn't willing to trust her oldest brother. Not yet.

"Can I start at the beginning?" Bear's haggard gaze shifted between the two of them.

"If you can do it in five minutes," Madison said.

"I'll do my best." He let out a deep breath and ran his hand down his beard. "I guess I can say all this now since Verna is dead."

"What does she have to do with any of this?" Confusion zinged through her thoughts.

"This all started with her. She kicked me out as

soon as I turned eighteen. She said if I tried to get in touch with you, that she would plant evidence to make me look like an accomplice to dad."

Madison tried to process what he said, but his words didn't make any sense. "Why would Verna want you out of the house so badly?"

"She was no longer receiving any government assistance for me. Just for the two of you." He pressed his lips together, his jaw twitching.

"Are you saying that the two of us were just a paycheck to her?" Surprise raced through Madison's voice—even though it shouldn't.

He shrugged, almost apologetically. "Unfortunately, yes."

Madison shook her head, still trying to comprehend this update. "Why did she try to keep you away?"

"I told her I was going to get guardianship of both of you." Bear shrugged. "She didn't like that idea."

"So, you just walked away?" Isaac stared at him, the judgment remaining in his voice.

Bear's gaze darkened. "Verna had this whole story concocted, including manufactured evidence to back it up. She wanted to make me look guilty and send me to prison. I have no doubt about that."

"What kind of evidence?" Isaac asked.

Bear frowned and rubbed his beard again. Finally, he let out a long breath. "It was an SD card from my camera."

Madison's heart thumped harder in her ears as she wondered where he was going with this. "What was on the card?"

"A video of one of the murders." His statement hung in the air.

Isaac stood and began pacing. "Wait . . . how did one of the murders get on your SD card?"

"I have no idea."

Isaac locked gazes with his brother. "You need to level with us, Bear. No more secrets."

"I am leveling with you. I have no idea how it got there."

"And you never thought to show this video to the police?" Isaac asked.

Bear rubbed a hand over his face, the emotional toll this conversation was having on him clear. "Verna showed it to me before I even knew it was on there. There was nothing on it that would have offered any additional clues. It would have only served to make me look guilty."

"Where is this SD card now?" Madison asked.

"Verna kept it and held it over my head as leverage. I have no idea what happened to it."

Isaac shook his head as if still hung up on some other details. "So, do you think the real killer planted that card in your camera to set you up? Otherwise, where did it come from?"

"I have no idea." Bear shrugged, a solemn look on his face.

But things suddenly made sense for Madison—all his years of being absent and distant.

*Verna* had done this to them.

She didn't for a moment believe that Bear had been behind those original murders. When the first one happened, he'd only been twelve; the last one when he was sixteen.

What sense did all of this make?

"After we were out of the house . . ." Madison started. "Why didn't you try to contact us then?"

"At that point, the two of you hated me. You thought I'd abandoned you. And I couldn't blame you for that. I accepted that this was the way it would be—for all our sakes."

"So you moved up here and just made a life for yourself as a hermit?"

He shook his head. "It wasn't that easy. I worked construction for several years until I saved enough to buy this place and pay for my schooling. In the meantime, I tried as much as I could to stay away from the people in town and their judgment. I tried to stay close to keep my eye on things. If Verna got too bad, I was willing to go to jail for you. But I also realized that if you went into foster care, then worse things could happen—worse than Verna."

Madison's head pounded. Could this really be the truth? Could this be what had happened, and Bear just hadn't told them before?

"I got my degree online and began to teach forensics. But all along, I've been searching for dad's accomplice."

"You still think Dad is guilty?" Isaac's voice hardened. "Even knowing what you do now?"

His tortured gaze flickered between Isaac and Madison until he finally nodded. "I knew Dad was leaving the house at night. When I asked him about it, he said it was nothing, that I shouldn't worry."

"That doesn't make him a killer," Madison said.

"No, but the fact that he won't tell us what he was really doing seals his guilt in my mind. If he were innocent, he would offer a reason. One night, I saw him return home. His shirt was rumpled. There was mud on his shoes. He looked like he'd just been in an accident or something."

"What did he say?" Isaac asked.

Bear's gaze darkened. "He told me to go back to bed. End of discussion. That's when I knew what he'd done. That's when I knew he was The Good Samaritan Killer."

# CHAPTER THIRTY-SIX

I LINGERED in the woods outside Bear Colson's again.

I just couldn't seem to help myself.

I'd tried to think up possible scenarios, possible ways I could insert myself into their discussions. What would they think if I showed up at the front door and pretended my car had broken down? Would they think twice about it?

I wasn't sure.

I couldn't do that. I couldn't let my curiosity win over my hunger to kill.

I crept closer—close enough that I could see inside the window.

Madison Colson sat on the couch, talking to her brothers.

She really was a remarkable woman. I'd known that when I watched the life fade from her. Something close to a sense of peace had washed over her features.

Peace?

That's when I knew I couldn't kill her. I needed to see her terrified first.

So, I'd compromised. I'd figured out another plan. A plan that would ensure she knew my power.

I couldn't wait to see her face up close again. To see the terror in her gaze. To watch the fight drain from her body as she succumbed to death.

I smiled.

Next time, she wouldn't look so peaceful.

And that next time was coming soon.

# CHAPTER THIRTY-SEVEN

FIRST THING THE NEXT MORNING, Isaac and Madison headed to the church to meet with the pastor about the next day's graveside service. They invited Bear to come along, but he'd insisted he had classes to teach.

Madison knew her oldest brother wasn't ready to honor Verna's life after what the woman had put him through, and Madison couldn't blame him. Part of her didn't want to honor Verna's life either. But she wasn't going to back out now—she simply wanted to get this over with.

As they drove to the church, her mind went back to the crosses she'd found. She'd wrestled all night with whether or not she should tell Shane about them. Part of her knew she should, that he'd be angry if he found out she didn't tell him. Another part of her believed her brother and wanted to protect his innocence.

If she told Shane, she'd just be giving the feds a false lead. Why waste their time?

But if that was the right choice, why did she feel so unsettled?

She frowned and continued to stare out the window.

Finally, she and Isaac pulled up to the church they'd grown up attending every Sunday morning and Wednesday evening. The white, traditional building with its steeple and church bell held good memories, despite the hard times they'd had in this town.

Pastor Brian Stephens met them inside to talk about the details of the service. After the arrangements had been worked out, Brian and Isaac veered into a conversation about football, so Madison began to wander through the familiar old building.

As she pushed through the swinging doors into the classroom wing, she nearly collided with someone. Madison jumped back and stared at the slight woman with blonde hair stretching nearly to her waist until Madison realized who she was.

"Rebecca Moreno?" Madison muttered almost breathlessly.

The woman stared back, her eyes widening with recognition. "Madison Colson? Oh, my goodness! It's been so long."

"It has been."

Rebecca had gone to school with Madison. She'd always been kind, even when others had kept their distance—even when Rebecca's own aunt had died at the hands of the Good Samaritan.

Then Rebecca's dad had forbidden her from talking to Madison's family. Not long after, Madison, Isaac, and Bear had transferred to the new school.

Rebecca hesitated only a second before pulling Madison into a warm hug. "I heard what happened to Verna. I'm so sorry."

"So are we. It's been complicated, to say the least."

Rebecca took a step back, her gaze warm. "I can't even imagine what you're going through."

Madison needed to change the subject before she broke down and told Rebecca all her problems. Rebecca was that type of person—the kind who was easy to speak with and open up to.

"By the way, what are you doing here?" Madison asked.

Rebecca glanced at the rooms lined along the hallway and smiled. "I volunteer here once a week. I just make copies and do a few things like that. No big deal, really."

"That's great. Isaac and I are just here meeting about the graveside service tomorrow."

Rebecca hiked an oversized bag up higher on her shoulder before casually crossing her arms over her chest. "How long are you in town? I would love to catch up. In fact, I thought about trying to get in touch when I heard you were here. But I realized I don't have your phone number."

"That would have been nice. My original plan was to leave after the graveside service, but I'm not a hundred percent sure yet."

As the swinging doors opened and Isaac stepped through, Rebecca's eyes widened.

"Isaac . . ." Rebecca stared at him, her voice suddenly husky.

"Rebecca . . . how are you?" Isaac paused in front of her, a sense of awe seeming to fall on him. "It's been a long time."

"Yes, it has. You look . . . great."

He looked her up and down. "So do you. I can't believe you're here."

"Never left. I've been taking care of Andi and Makayla."

"Andi and Makayla?" Isaac repeated.

"My cousins. Their parents died in a car crash a few years back, so they moved in with me and my father. I've mostly taken care of them, though. My dad . . . he's taken to drinking."

Realization seemed to wash over his face. "I see."

Madison was missing something here, and she wasn't sure what. She'd pepper Isaac with questions later when they were alone.

"Look." Rebecca pressed her lips together and ran a hand across her brow as if nervous. "This probably isn't my place to say it. But since I ran into you both now, it almost seems like a sign."

"What do you mean?" Madison asked, curious as to where she was going with this.

She stepped closer and lowered her voice. "I've heard about everything going on. I've heard about the videos that were online and then taken down. I didn't watch any of them myself. That seems too morbid. But I was in the diner two days ago . . ."

"Go on." Isaac stepped closer, curiosity evident in his gaze.

Rebecca squeezed her eyes shut as if she wasn't sure if she should continue. "I don't want to throw anyone under the bus. But this man was sitting in a booth watching those videos over and over again, and it just kind of freaked me out."

"Who was it?" Isaac asked.

Rebecca's gaze met Isaac's. "Harry Simpkins."

Madison sucked in a breath. "My dad's friend?"

Rebecca glanced around as if to make sure no one else was nearby before nodding. "He's the one."

MADISON FELT the anxiety bubbling inside her.

Could Harry be behind this? She didn't want to believe it was true. The man had always been so nice to them. But Madison couldn't afford to have blinders on right now.

"What are you thinking?" Isaac examined her face.

"My thoughts are all over the place. Should I tell Shane—Agent Townsend—about this?"

"Shane?" Isaac raised his eyebrows.

She instantly regretted her words. "Oh, stop. It was a slipup. Anyway, what do you think?"

His smile dimmed, and he let out a sigh. "It can't hurt to mention it to him. You know what else I want to do? I want to go to Verna's one more time."

"Why? We already searched for her will and Dad's papers."

"I want to see if we can find that SD card Bear mentioned."

"Won't that be like searching for a needle in a haystack?"

"Maybe. But we have to look. If the police find that . . ."

Dread filled her. Isaac didn't even have to finish that statement. He was right.

If the police got their hands on that, then Bear would definitely look guilty.

"Let's go."

A few minutes later, they pulled up to the house again. Madison would like to think it looked more inviting in the daylight, but it didn't. The place would never have good memories for her.

While Isaac checked Verna's dresser, Madison checked her nightstand again, looking beyond the bottles of lotion and packages of tissues.

"So, Shane, huh?" her brother said, almost as if he couldn't resist pestering her about the slipup.

"He told me I could call him that." She scowled, knowing exactly where he was going with this conversation.

"You two getting close?"

"I don't know if I'd say that. We're . . . we're working together. Even if Shane wanted something more—and I'm not saying that's the case—I'm not sure that could ever happen. I mean, think about the obstacles between us."

"Obstacles are meant to be overcome, right?"

His words almost sounded like a challenge. But she needed to change the subject. "Maybe. What about you and Rebecca? I noticed some tension there. What am I missing?"

Isaac's smile disappeared, and he searched more fervently through Verna's dresser. "We . . . we might have secretly been seeing each other during high school."

Madison paused and turned toward her brother, his unexpected words consuming all her attention. "Really?"

How could she not have known this?

"Rebecca's dad found out . . . and he was angry. I thought he might kill me. In fact, he threatened to kill me if he ever caught us together again."

"So you stopped seeing each other?"

Isaac shrugged, a melancholy look crossing his face. "I thought it would be better for all of us if I did."

Two things lingered in Madison's mind. First was

how sad it was for both Isaac and Rebecca that things had ended that way between them. Second . . . would someone—Rebecca's dad—be angry enough over what had happened to his sister to kill as revenge?

Before she could dwell on her questions too long, something slammed into the front of the house.

Madison froze and glanced at Isaac.

His expression had to mirror her own.

What if the killer had followed them here?

# CHAPTER THIRTY-EIGHT

"ISAAC . . ." Madison muttered.

"Stay there." His shoulders stiffened as he stepped toward the doorway.

She reached for him. "No! You don't have to check it out. Please . . . don't."

His gaze remained fixated on the direction of the sound. "What are we supposed to do then? Stay here like sitting ducks?"

"What if it's the killer?"

"Why would he bang on the window?" Isaac asked.

"To lure us outside? To let us know he's here? I don't know." She grabbed her phone. "I'm going to call Shane."

"Wait . . ." Isaac stepped closer to the sound. "We don't want to be like the boy who cried wolf."

"We don't want to be murdered at the hands of a merciless killer either." Her words came out rushed, colliding into each other as fear tried to conquer her.

"Good point." He peered around the door. "But . . . I see lights out front."

"Lights?"

He nodded. "Two sets of headlights."

What sense did that make?

Isaac crept closer, and this time Madison didn't stop him.

But as he reached the foyer, he let out an exasperated breath. "It's the media. If I had to guess, the sound we heard was one of them trying to get a glimpse inside the house. Let me go handle them."

The media? Madison let out a breath.

She'd take them over a killer any day.

"LET ME GET THIS STRAIGHT." Shane leaned back in his chair as Isaac and Madison sat with him at the sheriff's office in the conference room. "A friend of yours said Harry Simpkins was in the diner two days ago watching these Good Samaritan videos?"

"That's correct." Isaac nodded. "I wanted to share the update with you in case it's a viable lead."

Shane twisted his head. "That's interesting, but it's not enough to pinpoint him as a killer."

Madison leaned closer, fire blazing in her eyes. "I know that. But this guy has an affiliation with my family. He was close enough to my father that he would have been able to plant evidence."

Shane kept his gaze level with her. "Anything else?"

She leaned back and nibbled on her lip. "I always heard Mr. Simpkins had a temper. I had some friends who took his classes. He usually seemed mild-mannered. But, every once in a while, someone pushed his buttons and he lost it."

"There's no mention of that in his record."

"He didn't lose it as in hurt anyone," Madison continued. "But he'd yell at the students. My friend said she could see the anger simmering in his gaze."

Shane thought about it a moment before letting out a long breath. "It can't hurt to check him out. He should be at the school teaching right now, so maybe I can grab a few minutes of his time there."

"Can I go along?" Madison asked.

He stared at Madison a moment before nodding. "I guess there wouldn't be any harm in that."

"I have a few other things I need to do, if that's okay." Isaac rose from his seat, not quite looking like himself today. His usual confidence seemed to have faded, and his gaze made him appear troubled.

Had something happened that Isaac and Madison weren't telling him about?

"That's fine with me," Shane said. "I'll keep an eye on Madison."

"You don't have to babysit me, you know . . ." Madison gave him a pointed look.

"I know. But I don't want anything to happen to you either."

A few minutes later they were in his SUV riding down the road.

"Everything okay this morning?" he asked, then glanced at Madison.

She played with the ends of her hair as if she tried to sort out her thoughts. "I guess."

"Nothing else has happened?"

She shrugged, almost a little too quickly. "We're fine. Just a lot on my mind. A lot going on, and family problems on top of everything . . ."

"I can only imagine. Isaac didn't quite seem like himself either."

"I noticed. Something seems to have shaken him up."

Shane stored that information at the back of his mind.

The high school wasn't far away, and they pulled up to it a few minutes later. They walked into the office and paused near the front desk.

He showed his ID to the secretary, a fifty-something woman with curly blonde hair whose name badge read, "Gloria."

"FBI Special Agent Townsend. I need to talk to Harry Simpkins."

The woman pushed her pink, plastic-framed glasses up higher on her nose. "I'm sorry. Mr. Simpkins isn't in today."

Shane's spine stiffened. "Do you know when he'll return?"

"Let me check." The woman typed something into the computer before shrugging. "He took the rest of the week off."

The tension coursing through him grew stronger. "When exactly did Mr. Simpkins' leave start?"

"Two days ago." The woman's gaze flickered as she studied the computer screen.

"How far in advance did he put in for this time off?"

Gloria shook her head. "It was last minute. We had to scramble to find some subs. But Mr. Simpkins hardly ever takes any time off. I think he likes to stay busy since his wife died."

Shane nodded slowly, not believing in the coincidental timing. "Good to know. Thank you so much."

---

"DO you think Harry Simpkins took off work so he could enact these crimes?" Madison asked as soon as they were back in Shane's SUV.

"I think it's a good possibility. But it's too soon to draw any conclusions. I need to call my guys and see if we can track him down somehow. We'll look up his cell phone records. Talk to neighbors. See what we can find out. Maybe even get a search warrant."

Madison nodded. "I can't stand the thought of him being behind this. He was always nice to us growing up."

"He told me he wanted to adopt you and your brothers, but his wife wasn't in favor of it."

"That's the first I've heard of it. I think his wife died a few months ago."

"You never got any bad vibes from him?" Shane asked.

"No, he always seemed like a nice guy when he was around me." Madison let out a sigh. "What now?"

"I'm going to make those calls. Then I have a proposition for you."

"What's that?"

"I'd like to take you back to the cabin where you grew up and see if there's anything there that sparks any memories."

She felt the blood drain from her face at that prospect. She hadn't been back there in years. Certainly, seeing her childhood home would open old wounds.

But if that's what she needed to do in order to find answers, then she would.

# CHAPTER THIRTY-NINE

MADISON STARED at her childhood home.

The two-story log cabin had a tin roof stretching across the top.

When she was younger, the place had been neat and welcoming. Today, weeds grew wild in the yard. A screen hung halfway off a window. A couch had been dumped in the side yard.

But Madison didn't notice any of those things as much as she noticed the graffiti slashed on the front. The word "Killer" had been sprayed in red across the front door along with some obscenities.

No doubt this house had become an attraction for those obsessed with The Good Samaritan Killer. Some had come to gawk. Others to send a message.

"Are you sure you're up for this?" Shane stepped closer, his voice tender with concern.

She could feel the body heat coming from him and had to resist the desire to step closer, to see if she could catch a whiff of his leathery cologne.

Where were these thoughts coming from? This man was her enemy.

Except he wasn't.

He'd proven to her that he could be trusted—if she would loosen up enough to do so.

"As ready as I'll ever be." She held up the key in her hand. For some strange reason, she always kept it with her, even though she hadn't used it in years.

She drew in a deep breath as she stepped through the knee-high grass and toward the building. Maybe she should have paid someone to maintain the property. But she hadn't been able to bring herself to do that.

As soon as she unlocked the door, a noise sounded in the distance.

Shane turned, his body shielding hers as he looked out at the woods.

Her breath quickened. Was someone out there?

"Madison, go inside and shut the door."

She nodded so quickly that her head felt like it was spinning. The last thing she wanted was to be alone. But she knew she couldn't go trekking through the woods looking for a killer either.

She opened the door and slipped inside the dark cabin. As she shut it, she prayed Shane would be okay.

SHANE GRIPPED his gun as he stepped toward the woods. He'd definitely heard someone out there.

Was the killer here? Had he just been watching, waiting for Madison to return?

He had no idea.

Maybe this guy had been following Madison. Maybe he was just looking for the opportunity to strike again.

The thought didn't make him feel better.

Shane reached the edge of the woods and ducked between the trees.

The noise hadn't been far away.

But if this guy had his sights on Shane then Shane was in trouble. He had to remain vigilant.

He stepped forward, the crisp leaves crackling beneath his boots.

The landscape sloped only a few feet away. He had to be careful.

One wrong step would send him sliding down the mountainside. Craggy rocks and hefty boulders waited below.

He listened for a minute, hoping the man would make another sound.

There was nothing.

Was this guy waiting to ambush him?

Before going farther, Shane pulled out his phone and texted Brammall to let him know what was going on. He was going to need backup out here.

Slowly, he continued along the edge of the forest, looking for any signs of this guy.

But there was nothing.

Almost like no one had been here.

But Shane had definitely heard something. So had Madison.

He hadn't imagined it.

He needed to keep searching the forest until he found this guy.

This could be his one chance to finally end this all.

# CHAPTER FORTY

MADISON PRESSED herself into the door, hardly able to breathe. What was going on out there? She wanted to leave this space and go to the window to look. But the windows had been boarded, leaving the house in almost complete darkness except for a few slivers of light that crept through the cracks in the boards.

A shiver ran down her spine.

She turned away from the door as her gaze focused. The house was dark, but she could make out faint outlines of furniture.

She looked to the right, toward the staircase. She remembered running down it on Christmas morning to see what kind of gifts she had under the tree.

She remembered Isaac sliding down the banister, only to end up with four stitches in his head.

She remembered Bear using a broomstick as a sword and a towel as a cape as he pretended to be a superhero fighting evil.

Happy memories now marred by ugly ones.

Marred by images of the FBI showing up at the door. Roughly handcuffing her dad. Social services putting Madison, Isaac, and Bear in the back of the car until her aunt could pick them up.

Madison remembered the tears that had flowed down her face uncontrollably.

At eleven, she hadn't fully comprehended everything that happened.

Back in the present, she heard a creak.

Was this old house just settling? Or had the wind blown? Perhaps a critter had moved in.

She had no idea.

All she knew was that fear slithered down her spine. Any minute now, its invisible fangs would dig into her skin, their venom paralyzing her with fear.

Maybe being inside wasn't safer after all.

Maybe she should go back out there and take her chances.

Or maybe she was just being paranoid.

Madison decided she'd take her chances outside.

She turned toward the front door and her fingers scrambled to unlock it.

Before she could grab the handle, a figure rushed from the shadows.

A hand flew over her mouth, and an arm clamped over her midsection.

She tried to scream but couldn't as fear rushed through her.

"You're going to do as I say or I'm going to kill you. Do you understand?"

She recognized that voice.

It belonged to the man who'd tried to murder her three days ago.

Had he been waiting for her here?

Or had Madison just happened to stumble upon him?

It didn't matter. Not right now.

Because right now, her life flashed before her eyes.

WHOEVER HAD BEEN in the woods was gone.

Or maybe no one had ever been there at all.

Or . . . what if someone simply wanted to distract him? What if someone had thrown a rock as a misdirection?

And what if Shane had walked right into this person's plan?

His nerves tightened as he sprinted toward the cabin.

He needed to check on Madison. He thought he'd left her in a safe place.

What if he hadn't?

He darted up the rickety steps and shoved at the door, but it wouldn't budge.

"Madison!" He pounded his fist on the old wood.

When she didn't answer immediately, he kicked the door. It splintered, and sunlight flooded the musty space, revealing a place trapped in time.

But Madison was nowhere to be seen.

His heart beat harder.

"Madison?"

There was no answer, only the echo of his voice.

He gripped his gun and stepped deeper into the space, keeping his steps steady and his back to the wall. He couldn't be taken by surprise here.

But he didn't have any time to waste either.

He checked the living room.

It was empty.

The dining room.

Also empty.

As was the kitchen, bathroom, and closet.

There was only one place left in this house.

Shane stared at the steps leading to the second floor.

Was she up there?

Why would she have gone up there without him?

He knew the answer to that question.

She wouldn't.

Unless someone else had forced her.

# CHAPTER FORTY-ONE

TERROR RUSHED THROUGH MADISON.

With a knife at her throat, the man had pulled her up the stairs and into her old bedroom.

Images of the night he'd attacked her replayed in her head. As did the fear that came with it.

"You should have never come back here," he growled.

She wanted to speak. To scream.

But every time she even breathed, she felt the prick of the sharp blade against her neck.

Would he really do it this time? Would he kill her?

"Madison?"

Her breath caught at the distant voice.

Shane.

He was back in the house.

And in danger.

"I told you I wasn't done with you yet," the man whispered. "But I need to get this guy out of the way first."

As if right on cue, Madison heard a door open down the hall.

A crash followed, and someone moaned.

Her heart leapt into her throat.

Shane?

What had this guy done to him?

---

SHANE'S HEAD pounded as he sprawled on the floor.

He glanced beside him and saw rocks surrounding him.

He'd opened the bedroom door, and stones had cascaded from above. He'd tried to throw himself out of the way, but he'd still been hit.

He'd walked into a trap.

His gut clenched at the thought of it.

Where was Madison?

Just as the question raced through him, Madison rushed toward him. Worry was etched into the lines on her forehead, in the storminess of her gaze as she knelt at his side.

"Oh, Shane . . ." She touched the side of his face. "Are you okay?"

"I think." He pushed himself up farther, despite the pounding in his head. "You?"

She started to reach for her throat then stopped—but not before Shane saw something red. Had that guy cut her?

"I'm okay," she insisted, her voice hoarse. "But the man . . . he was here. He shoved me away as soon as he heard these rocks falling, and then he jumped out the second-story window."

Shane tried to stand. He needed to go after this guy.

But his head pounded too hard. There was no way he could chase anyone in his current state.

That had been the plan, hadn't it?

"Backup should be here any minute." He dragged himself to his feet, determined to push past this.

But, as he did, he wobbled and reached for the doorframe. Madison remained in front of him, her worried gaze on him as she slipped an arm around his waist for support.

"I can't believe he did that," she said. "It was almost like he knew we were going to come here."

"There's no way anyone could have known. We didn't decide to come here until today. We didn't even tell anyone."

"Maybe he just knew we would come eventually . . ." She nibbled on her lip and frowned.

He let out another soft moan as another ache pulsed through him. "Maybe."

"We need to have an ambulance here to check you out."

The last thing Shane wanted was for some medical issue to slow his investigation. But Madison was right. Head wounds had to be taken seriously.

With a sigh, he pulled out his phone again and requested paramedics on the scene.

## CHAPTER FORTY-TWO

WHILE SHERIFF WILDER and Brammall checked out the cabin, paramedics checked out Shane and Madison.

Everything still felt surreal to Madison. How had that even happened? Had this guy just been waiting for them to show up? If not, what had he been doing here?

The question made a shiver rush up her spine.

How could a house that was once so full of good memories now be such a place of nightmares?

She glanced at the fireplace and remembered happy Christmas mornings with stockings on the mantel and presents under the tree. She remembered having family and friends over after church on Sundays to share meals together and basketball games on the driveway out front. She remembered birthday parties with pointy hats and homemade cakes.

Not only was her childhood over, but sometimes it felt like her innocence had been erased also. Some memories were better left buried in the past.

Everything had changed when her dad was arrested. The hardest part about permanent changes was knowing there was no hope to make things right again. When a person gained weight there was always hope they could lose it. When a person lost a job, there was hope they could find a new one. When a relationship ended, eventually there was hope that someone new could be found.

But having her dad arrested and convicted of being a serial killer was something hard to come back from. She'd had to start life new and fresh. But that didn't mean she'd ever really let go of the baggage of what could have been.

That was too often what it felt like. Like Madison's family had drawn the short straw instead of having a nice, normal life. They'd been thrust into the outrageous.

She shook the thoughts from her head. Feeling sorry for herself would do nothing. All she could do right now was to look forward. That was what

Madison often told the people that she worked with. She needed to be certain to apply those words to herself also.

"Townsend." Brammall stopped in front of him. "I think we found something."

Shane stood from the couch where the paramedics were looking at his head. Suddenly, it appeared his own medical treatment was forgotten. "What is it?"

Brammall glanced at Madison before stepping closer to Shane, almost as if he didn't want her to hear.

"It's okay," Shane insisted. "Madison wants to help find whoever is doing this."

Brammall's neck tightened, but he nodded. "There were some cameras set up in the house, small ones you probably wouldn't notice unless you were looking."

Shane touched his head as it pounded harder. "Video cameras? Why would someone set up video cameras? Are they new or old?"

"They were new. Pretty high-quality. But there's more."

"Go on." Shane's hands went to his hips as he waited to hear the rest.

"The recordings were all sent to a feed on a

computer in a third bedroom upstairs. It looks like this guy was just waiting for you guys to come. He recorded the whole attack."

"That's because this guy gets his enjoyment out of recording everything he does and the shock value of it," Madison said. "This was all on purpose."

"We'll need to watch that video and see if we can pull anything off it," Shane said.

"We'll do what we can. We'll also see if we can track down who these cameras were sold to or if the serial number on the computer is linked with anybody."

"Don't get your hopes up, but it's only smart to check, just in case. But this guy seems to be intelligent and tech savvy."

Madison stored that information away. Shane was right. Whoever was behind this knew their way around a computer and a camera.

Did that match with any of the suspects that were already in her mind?

She wasn't sure.

But whoever was behind this was getting entirely too much pleasure out of the action.

AFTER SHANE HAD REVIEWED the footage—he hadn't seen anything remarkable on it, but it would be further analyzed by people at the field office—he took Madison to his SUV. He left his crew at the scene to continue searching for any other clues.

In the meantime, he needed to swing by the cabin he'd rented and take a quick shower before going back to work.

As they took off down the road, he explained what he was planning to Madison and asked if she wanted to go back to Bear's or go with him.

She shrugged. "I want to find this guy. I want to do whatever I can to help. So, if it's okay, I'll go with you."

"Of course." Shane was glad she'd said that. The realization surprised him.

He'd always known that the woman was attractive. But the more he was around her, the more his attraction seemed to grow.

Madison was more than a pretty face and more than a tortured soul. She could have taken what had happened to her and let it destroy her life. But she hadn't. Instead, she was a woman with compassion, integrity, and leadership—all qualities he admired.

Ever since he and Olivia had broken up, Shane

hadn't been interested in dating. In fact, he'd dedicated himself to his job.

Was it possible that something was changing inside him?

"This guy really gets too much pleasure from making these videos, doesn't he?" Madison's voice pulled him from his thoughts.

"My guess is that he watches the videos multiple times and feels the pleasure of the kill each time."

Madison stared out the window, almost looking stoic. "You still say this isn't the Good Samaritan?"

"I don't think it is. I think this guy is a copycat. But I think whoever is behind this has the same mindset and mental wiring as the killer. I think they both get pleasure from watching people suffer, out of pretending to be a hero and getting the praise while secretly killing people."

Madison turned toward him, a new light filling her gaze. "Maybe this is a crazy idea but hear me out. What if this person is a hero by day and a killer by night? Maybe that impulse is some kind of clue within itself."

"Keep going."

Madison's words came faster. "I don't want to point fingers at anyone who's not guilty. I'm just brainstorming here. But what if this guy is a sheriff's deputy or firefighter or in the military? Someone who's considered a hero? This person could love the rush of adrenaline he gets from the situation."

"I like where you're going with this."

"Obviously, this person also has a more sinister side. In fact, what if this person, on occasion on the job, may have had the opportunity to save somebody but instead killed them? What if no one ever knew about it?"

Shane's eyebrows rose as he stared at the road ahead. "That's a theory. It could have some merit. I'm going to have my guys look into it and see if there's anybody in this town that might fit that description."

"Do you think these crimes are confined to Fog Lake?"

"I can't say for sure. That seems like the most logical explanation since most of them have been committed within a twenty-mile vicinity. But our perp could be someone who frequents the town and commits other crimes in other places. There are a lot of unknowns right now."

Madison nodded, a new determination in her gaze. "I'd say."

Shane pulled to a stop in front of the small cabin he'd rented for himself and Brammall. He hadn't had many choices when he'd come into town. But this place had two bedrooms and was located in a relatively secluded area of Fog Lake.

He had to admit that he enjoyed stepping outside in the morning and admiring his view of the fog-covered mountains. He didn't have much time to enjoy the scenery—usually only while drinking his coffee. But the sight was a nice refresher before a hard day.

He climbed from the SUV and walked around to help Madison out. As they headed toward the front door, he scanned their surroundings, looking for anything suspicious.

As he did, a crash sounded in the distance.

He grabbed Madison and pushed her against the wall, using his body to shield her.

Then he glanced around, looking for whatever had caused that noise.

MADISON HEARD the noise and froze.

Was the killer here? Had he followed in order to exact more revenge?

Her throat tightened. The very thought of experiencing near-death again made her want to disappear. To crawl under a rock. To run.

To do anything but stay here and fight it out.

But those other things weren't an option.

Shane grabbed his gun as he scanned the woods as if preparing himself for a worst-case scenario.

Was the killer out there?

She held her breath as she waited. Her heart hammered into her chest.

Just then, a buck darted from the trees. He

leaped across the ground as he ran away, looking just as edgy as Madison felt.

Madison released her breath.

A deer. It was only a deer.

Thank goodness.

Shane holstered his gun before turning to her with a weary smile. "False alarm."

"That's a good thing, right?" Madison let out a shaky laugh.

"I think we're all on edge."

As Madison glanced up at Shane, she realized how close he was standing. She noticed the look in his eyes—hazy and filling with a desire that surprised her.

And thrilled her.

No, she couldn't desire him. She couldn't like somebody like Shane.

But she did, didn't she?

She'd thought she couldn't trust him. But the man had saved her life. He'd put her safety above his own. How could she fault him for that?

He reached up and trailed his finger along the side of her face, wiping the hair from her eyes. The feeling of his skin against hers made her knees feel weak.

The man was handsome and strong, and he was

running after integrity, trying his best to operate aboveboard.

Maybe he wasn't anything like his father. He'd proven that in the time since they'd gotten to know each other. But could Madison trust that wasn't all an act?

She wanted to. At least, right now she did.

His gaze dipped to her mouth, and then their lips met.

As the kiss consumed her, Madison clung to him. His hands reached around her waist and pulled her close. Her toes seemed to curl as time stood still. As all the pent-up emotions of the last several days were released in a gush of warmth and flutters.

She never wanted this moment to end.

When Shane pulled away, Madison's heart pounded in her ears. She felt unsteady—maybe even giddy.

She stole a glance up at him, almost afraid that kiss had been in her imagination.

Her tingling lips told her it wasn't.

That kiss . . . Shane had definitely swept her off her feet. Madison had forgotten about all her problems . . . for a moment. But the break had been nice. Very nice.

Shane still lingered close, his head tilted toward

her, and his body bent protectively to conceal her from any possible harm. His hands rested at her waist, and his breathing was heavy as if he needed to catch his breath.

Madison stared at his lips. They'd been surprisingly soft and yet firm with his skilled exploration.

She wondered what it would be like to kiss him again. To initiate the kiss this time. Would he let her take the lead? Or would he take control and leave her breathless again?

She hesitated, halfway wanting to find out and halfway knowing she shouldn't.

This was a bad idea. A very bad idea.

If she was a smart woman, she would end this before things went any further.

SHANE COULD HARDLY BREATHE AS he stood in front of Madison. He'd had no intentions of kissing her. But, in the heat of the moment, he'd let his guard down and given into his desires—something he rarely let himself do.

Madison had been standing there looking so vulnerable, so beautiful. So, he'd decided to throw caution to the wind and kiss her.

That kiss . . . it had been fantastic. Madison hadn't shown any hesitation as she'd clung to him, as she'd eagerly raised her lips to his.

"That was . . . nice." Madison's voice sounded breathless.

"Yes, it was." Shane still leaned in, his feelings growing stronger by the minute. Or maybe they'd been there already, and he'd simply been in denial. But the thought of almost losing her earlier today . . . it had done something to his heart.

Letting someone like Madison Colson walk out of his life would be a mistake.

Madison licked her lips as she stared up at him, her gaze showing the thoughts she had percolating inside.

"Shane . . . I think both of us know that the two of us together is a bad idea."

Shane withdrew slightly. "Right."

But even as the word left his mouth, he wasn't sure he believed it. Then again, he wasn't thinking very clearly right now.

"You're the man whose father put my dad behind bars," Madison said. "And I'm the girl who's trying to get my father out from behind bars. You still believe my father's guilty. I still believe he isn't. Once this case is over, we'll still be on opposite sides."

He stepped back even more, shoving his hands in his pockets. "I know. I don't know what came over me. I'm sorry—"

"Don't apologize." Madison's gaze locked with his, her eyes full of confidence and assurance. "It's just that . . . realistically speaking . . ."

"The two of us are incompatible," he finished.

She nodded quickly, almost regretfully. "Right. Incompatible. We could never make this work in the long run. For so many reasons."

Shane rubbed the back of his neck as he tried to get control of his thoughts. "It won't happen again."

Yet all he would think about was that kiss happening again and again.

He turned back to the door and opened it. "Come in. But let me check this place out before you get too comfortable."

Work. He needed to focus on work again.

Because focusing on Madison would only end with heartbreak.

# CHAPTER FORTY-FOUR

SHANE HAD INTENDED on taking Madison with him back to the sheriff's office if that was what she wanted. But, instead, Isaac had called and asked if they could go over some last-minute details for the graveside service tomorrow.

He dropped Madison off at Bear's house, instantly missing her when she was gone. Which was ridiculous. Because he had a job to do, and he couldn't let himself get distracted.

Forgetting about that kiss was the best thing he could do.

However, that would be easier said than done. Impossible, if he were to be honest with himself.

Halfway back to the station, Brammall called. "There's a new video."

Shane's back muscles tightened. "Another one?"

This guy wasn't wasting any time. How was it even possible that he was getting away with these murders so quickly?

"We haven't identified the victim yet," Brammall continued. "But I wanted to let you know so you could come into the station and look at the video yourself."

"I'm on my way right now. Tell me—how did he torture his victim this time?"

"Electrocution. It's . . . not pretty. One more thing. It appears this woman is wearing a college sweatshirt."

"Can you tell what college?"

"We think it's Wilshire University."

Shane's breath caught.

Wilshire? That was where Bear taught his online classes.

---

JUST AS LAST night before bed, Madison returned some phone calls and checked timely emails. She thought she'd be able get away from work for a few days, but it was more complicated than she'd expected.

Even if she wanted to stay in Fog Lake longer, it didn't appear she could.

She had clients who needed her. Paperwork was piling up. The list of phone calls she needed to return was growing.

Strangely enough, as many bad memories she had of this place, sometimes it felt like Fog Lake would always be home.

What would happen if her father was exonerated? Would she be able to show her face in this town again? Could their reputation be restored?

Did she even dare hope that might be possible?

Then there was Shane.

Why, in the short time since they'd known each other, had he made such an impact on her life? It was silly, really. The stuff dreams are made of. False realities.

How could the two of them share such a bond when they were on opposite sides of this fight?

Except... were they?

She wasn't sure sometimes. Things were never that simple, especially when emotions were involved. And life was full of surprises. Who knew what was going to happen next?

She sank down farther in bed, dreading tomorrow.

Madison would put on a brave face and honor Verna's life.

But she wasn't looking forward to it.

# CHAPTER FORTY-FIVE

TOMORROW WAS THE BIG DAY.

I practically salivated at the thought.

Timing could be everything. Especially when cooking. If each dish wasn't prepared at the right time, the serving temperatures would be messed up. The feast would be ruined.

And I couldn't allow that to happen.

Not after all the trouble I'd gone through.

It was time to get the ultimate revenge.

I stared at the picture in my hands.

The picture of Madison Colson. The source of my trouble. The one who'd stirred to life this desire to kill again.

It all went back to her.

Did she even know that?

Did the cops or the feds have a clue?

Those feds thought they were so smart. They weren't. That's why I wanted to toy with them, so I could let them know I was smarter. The cameras had been fun to set up. I'd stolen them from a town forty minutes away and put them in the house, knowing Madison would eventually go back there.

I was lucky. I'd been there when she'd arrived, and then I'd distracted that fed by throwing a rock into the woods.

But it wasn't her time to die yet. That was the only reason I'd let her go.

Speaking of which, the crosses were a nice touch.

Soon, there would be another cross.

The cross on Madison Colson's tombstone.

I smiled at the thought.

I could hardly wait to get started.

## CHAPTER FORTY-SIX

THE NEXT MORNING, a sense of melancholy fell over Madison as she stared in the mirror at herself in her black dress and heels.

With Aunt Verna dead, Madison had no excuse to ever come back to Fog Lake again. Not that she was looking for a reason.

But today's service signified the end of that chapter in her life. The end of that book, to be precise.

Today, Madison would put on a polite face as she stood by the graveside and tried to honor her aunt's life—even if it was the last thing she wanted to do, especially after what her aunt had done to Bear.

Aunt Verna's actions were inexcusable.

With one more glance at herself, Madison

straightened the edges of her dress and stepped from the spare bedroom.

As she walked into the kitchen, her eyes widened when she saw the strange man standing there.

No, not a strange man.

Bear.

He'd shaved, put on a suit, and looked like an entirely different person.

"Bear . . . you look . . . amazing. Respectable," Madison murmured. "But I didn't think you were going to the service."

He shrugged in his trademark solemn way. "I'm not going for her. I'm going for you and Isaac."

Warmth filled Madison. Maybe the two of them really were making some progress. Could their relationship be restored?

She hoped so.

"Thank you," she told him softly.

"Of course." A soft grin tugged at his lips.

Before she could say any more, Isaac clanked downstairs, paused beside Madison, and gaped.

"There's a clean-cut guy hibernating behind that beard, huh? I feel like I have my old big brother back." He punched Bear on the shoulder. "Looking good, man."

"Yeah, yeah, yeah." Bear shrugged again, making it clear he didn't want a big deal to be made of him.

But Madison couldn't help but smile at his transformation. Did the outward change signify something was changing on the inside also? She wasn't sure.

She grabbed her purse. "I guess we should get going."

"Let's get this over with," Isaac added.

"Ditto," Bear said.

---

MADISON and her brothers stepped outside into the crisp, fall day. Gray clouds hung overhead, and the wind felt brisker than it had earlier in the week. It was just strong enough to tug the leaves from the trees and send them flying through the air.

Soon, the forest would be bare.

Madison didn't quite feel ready for fall to be over yet.

As they started down the road in Isaac's car, her mind went back to that kiss last night with Shane. Madison didn't want to keep thinking about it, but she couldn't seem to stop herself. Every time she closed her eyes, she remembered just how sweet it had been. Maybe sweet wasn't the right word.

Passionate would be more like it.

It was best if she just forgot it happened. But that was easier said than done.

"What happens after today?" Bear asked. "Are you two going back to your regularly scheduled lives?"

Madison glanced at Isaac in the front seat, anxious to hear his answer. She wasn't sure about her own. When she'd come here, she had fully intended to leave as soon as possible.

But now there was a killer on the loose. Somehow it didn't feel right to leave without resolution. What if this went on for months? It wasn't like Madison could stay in Fog Lake indefinitely.

"I have that high-profile case I'm working on back in Memphis," Isaac said. "I don't know if I'll leave today. But maybe tomorrow. Coming back here has certainly stirred up a lot of memories."

Something about Isaac's words made Madison think that this would probably be the last time he ever came here also. She couldn't blame him. In fact, she understood.

"I'm not sure what I'll do either," Madison finally said. "I won't leave today. Maybe tomorrow. Or maybe I'll stay a while longer. With these new murders..."

She couldn't finish her statement, but she didn't need to. Certainly, her brothers knew exactly what she was talking about.

Last night, when she'd arrived back, she'd told them what happened at their childhood home. They'd both been horrified as she recounted the details. She'd also mentioned that another video had surfaced.

"What about you, Bear?" Madison asked. "You seem pretty content to stay here. You practically have your own little homestead."

He shrugged. "This is my home, and I won't let anyone drive me away. Besides, I like being by myself. I work hard to be self-sufficient."

Madison softened her voice before saying, "But, don't forget that we all need people in our lives, especially when the going gets tough."

"I know." Bear's voice held no trace of doubt. "But I'm okay."

Madison had to wonder if his words were true. Did Bear only *think* he was okay? If he knew what it was like to be fully involved in the lives of others, would he realize how much he was missing?

Maybe it was Madison's fault. Maybe she should

have tried harder to stay in touch with him. If she had, would he be living like a hermit right now?

She didn't know the answers, nor could she make decisions for him. Bear was a grown man fully capable of making his own choices. She'd be much better off to remember that.

SHANE RUBBED his hand over his face as he climbed from his SUV in the parking lot near the church cemetery.

He and his team had worked for much of the night, trying to track down clues from the video they found. They were able to match the woman's picture with the images from the video. They'd learned the victim was Alexandria Leonard, a nineteen-year-old college student.

Her roommate had said Alexandria hadn't returned to the dorm for the past two nights and wasn't answering calls.

It happened that Alexandria Leonard was taking one of Bear Colson's online classes.

Shane's lungs tightened at that thought.

What if Bear was the one behind this? A lot of boxes could be checked for him as a suspect. The most obvious was his relationship with James Colson. Bear would have been old enough at the time of the later murders to have assisted his father.

Not only that, but the man was a loner with forensic knowledge, he was connected to their latest victim, and his knife had shown up in a video.

Nothing definitively proved he was the one behind these crimes. But, during the graveside service, a team would be at Bear's house with a warrant investigating. Madison had mentioned that Bear wouldn't be at the service, but there was no good time to really check his home, and the sooner they did it, the better.

Shane would let Madison and Isaac get through this service before he told them.

He wanted to be here in case anyone of interest came.

And he wanted to be here, in part, to see Madison. To be there for her.

Shane knew Madison had said things would never work between them, and he was inclined to agree with that statement. Yet another part of him couldn't get the woman out of his mind.

That led to only one conclusion: trouble.

He pulled his jacket tighter around him as he joined the small crowd at the edge of the grave. Fog had settled between the headstones, creating an eerie feel—one that seemed appropriate for a funeral and for this town.

Madison offered a soft smile before looking back toward the coffin in front of her.

She looked lovely in a fitted black dress and her hair swept up into a twist. A black-and-white scarf adorned her neck—effectively covering her injuries—and she held a matching black purse in her hands.

She was the picture of classy and demure.

His pulse quickened just looking at her.

As Shane's gaze traveled to the other attendees, he did a double take at the men on either side of her. Isaac looked the same. But Bear . . . he looked like a completely different person.

He'd shaved, revealing a surprisingly clean-cut face.

Then another thought hit him. What if this guy had shaved because of ulterior motives? What if something happened in the middle of an attack and *that* had made him cut off his beard?

Maybe it was nothing, but Shane couldn't stop thinking about the question. What had Bear's motivation been to change his looks as he had? And why had he decided to come to the service?

Shane glanced at his watch and saw they only

had a couple more minutes until the service started. His investigative team should be in the thick of things by now.

He frowned.

Instead of concentrating on the search, he scanned the crowd.

Madison, Isaac, and Bear were quiet as they waited for the service to begin.

Verna hadn't exactly been the life of the party or a ray of sunshine, according to what he'd learned about her. But a faithful few had turned up to show their respects.

Tires crunched on gravel in the lot. Shane watched as a car skidded to a stop, the driver going entirely too fast.

A woman scrambled out and slammed the door. She yanked an oversized purse over her shoulder before hurrying toward the service.

Her eyes were red, and mascara drizzled down her cheeks. Her blonde hair, cut to her shoulders, bounced as she walked, and her black dress looked expensive.

Shane had never seen this woman before. So, who was she?

That's when he heard Isaac mutter, "Kate?"

# CHAPTER FORTY-SEVEN

MADISON SUCKED in a breath when she saw Kate rushing toward the group gathered at the grave. Something about the woman didn't look right. Maybe it was . . . her eyes.

Why was Kate crying for Verna, a woman she'd never met? Was she simply emotional? Maybe funerals were hard for her.

Madison didn't know.

Kate scurried toward Isaac and practically collapsed into his arms. Her chest heaved as she cried, and she murmured something loud but indecipherable into his chest.

"Oh, Isaac . . ." Her voice trailed off into sobs.

Her brother seemed to freeze before snapping

out of his daze and patting her back. "Kate . . . I didn't know you were coming."

"I had to support you. I'm so sorry you've been going through this alone. No one should be by themselves at a time like this."

"I'm not alone. I have my brother and sister." Isaac opened his mouth and shut it again, as if rethinking his next words. Finally, he said, "You really didn't have to come all this way."

Something about the way Isaac said the words made Madison think he hadn't *wanted* her to come.

Kate continued clinging to him, crying as the service started.

Kate may have been the only one who shed any tears. Everyone else simply listened solemnly as Pastor Brian talked about Verna.

Madison wanted to tune out everything he said. She didn't want to hear any accolades. Didn't want to pretend the woman was a saint.

In fact, the service couldn't end soon enough.

At the pastor's urging, Madison threw her rose on top of the casket. After a prayer, everyone was dismissed. The cemetery staff would take care of the rest.

As Bear began talking to Rebecca, Madison walked toward Shane. Her heart let out an involuntary flutter as she did. He looked handsome in his crisp black suit and bright blue tie that matched his eyes. His beard, as always, was neat and trim, just like his hair.

Why did this man have to be so handsome?

She paused in front of him, her breath frosting as she released the air from her lungs. "Thank you for coming."

"Of course." His words sounded gentle and sincere.

"How are you doing this morning?" But what Madison really meant was: are there any updates?

Shane seemed to know that.

A shadow filled his gaze. There *was* an update, wasn't there? But he was being polite and not telling her out of respect for the moment.

"We need to talk later," he murmured.

Part of her wanted to demand an answer. But Shane was right.

This wasn't the time or place. She needed to talk to the other guests who'd come to pay their respects.

But Madison's mind stayed on that look she'd seen in his eyes. What exactly did he know?

SHANE WATCHED as Madison greeted each attendee, smiling with grace and elegance.

He was impressed.

And it took a lot to impress him.

Her aunt hadn't been loving or warm. Yet Madison was honoring her life anyway. She was doing the right thing even when she didn't feel like it, and that to him was the picture of integrity.

Shane couldn't take his eyes off her. He only wished they'd met in different circumstances.

As he stood at the edge of the small group of attendees, his phone rang.

Brammall.

His stomach squeezed as he stepped away to answer.

"You'll never believe what we found at Bear Colson's place," Brammall started.

Shane's stomach squeezed harder. "What?"

"Silver crosses. Lots of them. And they're all similar to the ones our killer uses."

Shane's gaze traveled through the crowd before stopping on Bear.

Was this guy the one who'd been behind this the whole time? First, the knife. Then his association with Alexandria Leonard. Now crosses.

"One other thing," Brammall continued. "When

our team was searching Alexandria's dorm room, we found a handwritten note from someone telling her to meet him at 11:30 at Falls Ridge. That's an overlook outside of Fog Lake."

"And?"

"The handwriting appears to match Bear Colson's."

One thing was for sure: They finally had enough evidence to bring him in for questioning.

Shane hated to do it here. But the sooner they got this killer off the streets, the safer this whole town would be.

# CHAPTER FORTY-EIGHT

MADISON RUSHED toward Shane as he handcuffed Bear. "What do you think you're doing?"

Shane's voice sounded professional and cold as he addressed her. "We have evidence pointing to your brother as the copycat killer."

She gaped. "That's not possible. He's not the one behind this. You know he isn't."

"We found crosses at his house, just like the ones from the crime scenes." Shane's gaze caught hers.

Madison opened her mouth but shut it again, unsure what to say. But in that moment, realization swept through Shane's gaze. He sensed that Madison already knew about the crosses—just like she'd known about the knife.

Betrayal and accusation stained his gaze. "You

already knew, didn't you? But you didn't think it was important enough to tell me?"

"It's complicated." She crossed her arms.

Shane shook his head and began leading Bear toward his SUV, his disappointment evident. "There's nothing complicated about withholding evidence."

"Shane . . ." Desperation welled in her. Madison had to make him understand. She needed to explain!

But it was too late. Madison already felt the wall coming up between them.

"What's going on here?" Isaac joined them, his gaze flickering between Bear, Shane, and Madison.

Kate followed on his heels, almost as if she were a magnet who couldn't escape his pull. Several graveside service attendees also turned toward them as if curious about what was going on.

"The feds think Bear's guilty," Madison rushed.

Fire ignited in Isaac's eyes. "We're not going to let them do this to you, Bear—just like they did it to Dad. Don't say anything without me. I'll be right behind you."

"I didn't do this." Veins popped out on Bear's neck.

"We know you didn't." Isaac turned to Kate,

pushing her hands off his arm as if she'd trapped him. "I'm sorry, but I need to go."

"Let me go with you—"

Isaac turned back toward her, urgency in his motions—along with a touch of impatience. "Kate, I can't keep doing this. Thank you for coming all the way here for the graveside service. But you shouldn't have. We've talked about this before."

Tears flooded her eyes again. "But we're supposed to be together. You know it."

Isaac grasped the side of her arms. "I wish that were true. I really do. But I need you to understand that the two of us aren't going to work out. I'll always be there to support you. I'll always be your friend. But I can't be your boyfriend. I'm sorry."

"But . . ." Desperation claimed Kate's voice.

"Come on, Madison," Isaac called. "We have to get down to the station."

She paused long enough to glance at Kate. Her heart went out to the woman as she stood there looking devastated with her red eyes, streaky mascara, and knotted forehead.

But Madison's brothers needed her now.

Madison offered Kate a faint smile before rushing after Isaac.

She'd have to find out some answers about that situation later.

Right now, she needed to make sure Bear didn't go to prison, just like her father had.

---

SHANE COULDN'T BELIEVE Madison hadn't told him about the crosses in Bear's house. The realization dominated his thoughts as he headed back to the sheriff's office. But he had to let it go—for now—and focus on his job.

Bear sat in the backseat of his SUV, staring solemnly out the window.

Isaac had instructed Bear not to talk to the feds without his lawyer present. But Shane decided to ask him some questions on the drive anyway.

"How well did you know Alexandria Leonard?" Shane asked.

"Who's Alexandria Leonard?"

"Don't play dumb. This game is going to be over soon."

"I'm not playing any kind of game," Bear said. "If anything, someone is setting me up."

Shane had heard that excuse before. "If someone

is setting you up then they're doing a *really* good job."

Bear said nothing.

But Shane had a hard time believing that was the truth. Everything pointed to Bear. *Everything.* Maybe his father had trained him.

Except wouldn't he have told him about the GS carved in each of the previous victims?

Shane frowned at the thought.

He'd think about that later.

He turned his attention back to Bear, ready to drive home his final point. "What I don't understand is how you could do this to your sister, your own flesh and blood. Hasn't Madison been through enough?"

"I didn't do anything to Madison." Anger hardened the edges of Bear's voice. "I would *never* hurt her."

Shane had gotten to him.

But he wasn't sure Bear's words were true. In fact, the more time that passed, the more certain he felt that Bear was guilty of these crimes.

Shane needed to resolve this and put this case to rest once and for all.

Then he'd head back home to Knoxville and get away from this town and . . . Madison Colson.

# CHAPTER FORTY-NINE

MADISON PACED the lobby in the sheriff's office as she waited for an update from Isaac. An hour had passed since he'd gone in with Bear.

Nausea swirled in her, and she feared she might throw up at any time now.

Maybe she was having some type of post-traumatic stress moment. A moment where she remembered all too well what it was like when her dad was arrested. How everything had changed afterward.

Would everything change after this as well? Would her brother be tried and convicted?

Madison swallowed hard, pushing down the bile that wanted to rise up.

Instead, she pressed her eyes closed. *Lord, please be with Bear. Be with Isaac and help him to give wise counsel. Be with me and help me handle this well. Be with Shane. Help him see my brother isn't guilty.*

*I'm begging you, Lord. I can't go through this again. I can't.*

She opened her eyes and drew in a deep, calming breath.

As the door behind her opened, Madison turned and saw a woman rush into the lobby.

Madison blinked several times as the figure came into view. But when she realized who it was, her stomach only roiled more.

Kate . . .

What was she doing here?

The woman's gaze stopped on Madison, and she rushed toward her. Kate's face still looked flushed, and her eyes were red with tears. But she had wiped off the mascara streaking her face.

Comforting her brother's ex-girlfriend was the last thing Madison wanted to do right now. She had enough problems of her own. But . . .

"Where's Isaac?" Kate rushed as she glanced around the room.

"He's in with Bear."

Her face fell as if she'd expected to walk in and talk to him. "I'm sorry to hear that. I just wanted another minute with him."

Madison stared at Kate, who was clearly distraught. No one could mistake that. While Madison didn't want to dive into the middle of her brother's romantic drama, this woman appeared to need a listening ear.

She swallowed hard before asking, "Do you want to talk?"

Kate dabbed her eyes again. "Oh, Madison . . . I love your brother so much."

"It seems that way."

"It's just the stress of the situation. And his cases. The two of us . . . I just can't imagine my future without him."

"I don't know what happened between the two of you." Madison placed her hand on Kate's arm, trying to calm her down. "And I don't know whether your future is with Isaac or with someone else. . . but if it's *not* Isaac then there's somebody else out there for you."

She manically swung her head back and forth. "But there's not. It's only Isaac."

Madison somehow had to get through to her. "My boyfriend and I broke up several months ago, and it felt like the end of the world for a while. But it wasn't. I'm okay now. You'll be okay too."

"You can't know that. You can't." Kate's voice rose with every word.

Madison shushed her as people began to glance their way. "I don't know what else to say, Kate. I'm sorry that you're hurting. Is there a friend that you could stay with?"

"No. There's no one! Only Isaac."

"Kate . . ."

"You just don't understand!" Kate rose and stormed from the station just as quickly as she had come in—like a whirlwind.

Madison's gaze trailed behind her.

What in the world had happened to Kate? The last time they'd met the woman had seemed so happy. Isaac had seemed so happy. Obviously, there was more to the story.

In different circumstances, Madison might try to help more. But, right now, she needed to concentrate on Bear.

SHANE WASN'T GETTING any answers from Bear —mostly because Isaac had told the man to be quiet.

But that wasn't what they needed right now.

They needed to find Alexandria.

Frustration rose inside him with each moment of silence that passed. He'd tried everything to get him to talk. But Bear, who was normally stoic, remained that way now.

The only thing that planted doubt about his guilt in Shane's mind was the timeline.

If Alexandria had disappeared last night, was it physically possible that Bear was responsible? Or did he have an alibi?

Isaac and Madison had been staying with him. Certainly, they would have heard something if he'd left in the middle of the night.

Finally, Shane rose and stepped back. They could hold Bear for forty-eight hours without charging him. It looked like that was what they were going to end up doing unless they could find answers that were more than circumstantial.

As Shane stepped back into the hallway, Wilder approached him. "This could be nothing, but I just got a call from Ted Russo. He spotted a woman that meets Alexandria's description."

Shane's breath caught. "What? Where?"

"Sitting on a park bench at the edge of town. Alive."

Hope soared inside Shane.

He rushed toward the door. "I'm going to go

check it out."

If this was Alexandria and she'd survived the attack...

Could she identify the man who had done this to her?

# CHAPTER FIFTY

ISAAC EMERGED from the interrogation room.

He needed water, and he wanted to give Madison an update on Alexandria. As far as he knew, Madison hadn't heard there was a new victim.

As soon as he stepped into the lobby, she rose, questions filling her gaze. "Well?"

"It sounds like the feds have a lot of evidence against Bear. The knife is a smoking gun, for sure. But a new woman went missing, and she's one of Bear's students. That gave the feds enough probable cause to grant a search warrant on his home. When they went inside, they found the crosses."

"Another victim?" She shook her head. "That's horrible. Do you think they're going to charge him?"

"They have forty-eight hours to figure that out.

Right now, the evidence is all circumstantial. But I just saw Agent Townsend rushing out, and that makes me wonder what he knows."

"I saw that too. It almost seems like they have another lead." Her lips tugged down in a frown. "I can't believe another woman was taken."

"I know." Isaac lowered himself into the seat beside her. "Me either. This is just a nightmare."

"How's Bear?"

Isaac shrugged. "You know Bear. He's hard to read."

Madison studied Isaac's face, clearly searching for the truth. "You don't think he did this, do you?"

Isaac didn't hesitate before shaking his head. "No, I don't. I don't care what anyone says. Are you holding up okay out here?"

"I guess." She nibbled on her lip for a moment before saying, "Kate came by."

Dread filled him. "She did? What did she say?"

"That the two of you are meant to be together. She didn't sound like she was quite right in the head. I know it's none of my business, but what's going on?"

Isaac let out a long breath. He'd hoped to put that part of his life behind him. But that didn't appear to be happening.

"I've known for months that Kate isn't the one for me," he started. "I've tried to break things off with her on more than one occasion, but, every time I do, she has an episode."

Madison narrowed her eyes. "What do you mean by an episode?"

Bad memories pummeled him. "She makes a scene and will start crying hysterically. She tries everything she can think of to convince me that we were meant to be together."

"And that works?"

Isaac let out another breath. "The thing is . . . Kate has some problems. I didn't realize it until we were deep into our relationship. But I'm nearly certain she suffers from some depression and manic behaviors. She won't see a counselor about it. I've tried to encourage her, but she refuses. She won't get help."

Realization spread over Madison's features. "So, you're afraid if you break up with her, she's going to do something drastic?"

He slowly bobbed his head up and down. "That's my fear. But I can't stay with her forever, and I can't marry her because I feel sorry for her."

Madison's gaze held affirmation. "You're right. Dating is when you figure out if you're compatible or not. It sounds like breaking up with her was the right thing."

"It *feels* like the wrong thing. Feels like I'm the only one she has, and I'm afraid she's going to do something stupid." His shoulders pinched as the burdens of the past several months weighed on him.

"I'm so sorry, Isaac. Kate does need help. But she has to accept it first. You can't force it on her."

"Tell me about it." He let out a long breath. The last thing he needed right now was for Kate to add to the rest of his troubles.

"When can you see Bear again?" Madison glanced at her watch.

"I should probably get back in there. This certainly isn't the way I thought I'd be spending today."

"Me either. I thought maybe you, me, and Bear could sit down and have a meal together, maybe feel like a normal family for a moment." Hope faded from her voice.

Isaac let out a cynical chuckle. "That hasn't happened in a long time, has it?"

"No, it hasn't."

He stood and stretched his back. "Let me go check on Bear. In the meantime, stand by."

SHANE STARED at the young woman sitting on a park bench on the edge of town.

A blanket was wrapped around her shoulders, and her face looked pale as she stoically stared ahead.

But with her long, dark hair and olive skin, she definitely looked like Alexandria Leonard.

He paused and knelt until he was eye level with her. The woman was obviously shaken, and Shane didn't want his stance to intimidate her.

He studied her eyes, but they looked glazed and distanced. Shock, no doubt. Most likely, she'd also been drugged just like Madison.

"She's not talking," the deputy said. He'd remained with her until Shane could arrive.

"She hasn't said anything?" Shane questioned.

"Nothing."

Shane turned back to the woman, determined to see if she would talk. "My name is Special Agent Shane Townsend. Can you tell me your name?"

She didn't seem to hear him. Instead, she continued rocking on the bench as she stared blankly into the distance.

Shane quickly scanned her for any signs of

injuries. Bruises had formed on her neck. Her eyes were bloodshot. Her hair matted.

But otherwise, he didn't see any life-threatening injuries.

Isaac held up his phone with Bear's picture on it. "Do you know this man?"

Just for an instant, Alexandria's eyes seemed to focus. Then they glazed again, and she continued to rock.

As an ambulance pulled up, two paramedics rushed out to help. The woman definitely needed to be checked. Her safety was their first priority. Given the fact she wasn't talking, Shane didn't have any hopes of getting answers from her right now.

He'd send someone to the hospital to collect her clothing and see if any evidence had been left on her. Maybe a hair so they could get DNA from it. Maybe *Bear's* hair with DNA.

But this killer was probably smarter than that.

Then again, this killer wasn't the real one, so maybe he'd messed up.

Shane could hope, at least.

# CHAPTER FIFTY-ONE

AS MADISON LINGERED in the lobby, she couldn't stop thinking about what Isaac had just told her about Kate.

His words made more pieces fall into place, and a better picture formed in her mind of what his relationship with Kate was like.

Isaac was in a tough spot, one that Madison didn't envy. But she truly thought he'd done the right thing by breaking up with Kate. Madison wished she could get Kate the help she needed before this spun out of control.

Madison's thoughts shifted back to Bear. She hadn't learned anything new about him or the investigation. She prayed the feds would see that he wasn't guilty.

From what she understood, authorities were going to put Bear into a holding cell tonight. No doubt, they were trying to track down any evidence they could find so they could officially charge him on multiple counts of murder and assault.

She pressed her eyes shut and lifted another prayer at the thought.

Isaac emerged, looking more tired than Madison had ever seen him. He placed a hand on her back and led her out to his car. "We should go and try to get some rest. There's nothing else we can do here."

She didn't want to nod. Didn't want to agree.

What Madison wanted to do was to find the real killer so her brother could be released. If only it were that simple.

They climbed in the car, neither with much to say as they started back to Bear's place.

As they did, Madison glanced at her phone and saw she'd missed several messages.

Including one from Belinda Cox.

**Please call me ASAP. It's about Wayne. I don't know what to do.**

Madison frowned.

Wayne had killed his entire family except for

Belinda. The defense had blamed it on an unhealthy medication cocktail his doctor had put him on. Since the man didn't have a prior record, he'd been sentenced to a mental institution and charged with involuntary manslaughter instead of first-degree murder.

Madison would call Belinda when she got back to Bear's. Service was too spotty on this road. But she prayed that everything was okay.

Just as they reached a hairpin turn, a truck appeared on the winding road in front of them.

In their lane.

Heading straight for them.

Madison swallowed back a scream as time turned to gel.

"Isaac!"

He jerked the wheel but there was no time to avoid a collision.

As she tried to brace herself, the truck smashed into them.

Metal screeched.

Glass shattered.

Airbags exploded.

Pain coursed through her limbs.

Then everything went black.

# CHAPTER FIFTY-TWO

SHANE FELT UNSETTLED, to say the least. And he couldn't pinpoint why.

It was about more than the realization that innocent women had died and that more innocent women could be harmed if they didn't find this guy soon.

Alexandria still wasn't speaking. Shane had gone to the hospital himself to try to interrogate her, but it had done no good. The doctors didn't know when, or if, she'd come around and talk again. If she did, she might not even remember the trauma.

The crew investigating the incident with Susan Roseland hadn't turned up anything either. They'd searched the cliff she'd fallen from for any clues, but so far hadn't had any luck.

Now, with more FBI agents on the scene, they had more manpower to study the security camera footage, talk to witnesses, and warn the public to be more vigilant.

SAC Ross was coming down himself tomorrow to make a statement to the media. Worry about what was happening had definitely spread.

As he passed the conference room trying to sort his thoughts, Shane's mind flashed through everyone they had considered as a suspect.

Ted Russo.

Harry Simpkins.

Arnie Siebert.

Cap.

And, finally, Bear Colson.

He seemed like the most likely suspect.

But there was something bothering Shane. All these crimes seemed to be centered on Madison.

The feeling he got after talking to Bear was that he'd never want to harm his sister. Plus, they were still checking his alibi. There was a chance he was teaching during the time of some of these attacks.

What was Shane missing?

If he didn't figure it out soon, more people would be hurt.

He couldn't let that happen.

MADISON TRIED to pull her eyes open, but her eyelids were heavy. So heavy.

Her ears rang, the tone so sharp. She wanted to silence it. But she couldn't.

Something sticky plastered the side of her face.

And her entire body ached—even her teeth.

She tried again to pull her eyes open, but a cry escaped instead.

Then everything flashed back to her.

Driving down the road with Isaac.

The truck with the blinding headlights.

The crash.

Her pain was nearly forgotten as terror blindsided her.

She'd been hurt. Was she in the hospital right now?

No. If she were, she'd smell antiseptic. She'd hear beeps. Hear feet rushing in the hallway.

Here, all she heard was quiet—and that terrible ringing in her ears.

*You can do this, Madison. Just open your eyes. See where you are.*

But another part of her didn't want to know.

Reality nipped at the edge of her consciousness —a reality she wasn't prepared to face.

"I see you're finally coming to," a deep voice said above her.

The breath left her lungs at the sound.

She'd heard that voice before.

She knew exactly when.

When she'd almost died, and again when she'd visited her childhood home.

The Good Samaritan Killer—or his copycat— was with her now.

In fact, he'd caused that crash.

Madison had no doubt about it.

Another thought startled her with enough force that she tried to sit up. But she couldn't. Her muscles screamed. Her limbs felt like anchors. Her head . . . it hurt so much.

Instead, she pressed herself back down into the cushions beneath her and willed her muscles to relax.

*Isaac.*

Her throat swelled until she felt like she couldn't breathe.

Where was her brother?

What if he was . . . ? A cry escaped.

What if he was *dead*?

The agony that filled her chest almost made her want to die.

Not Isaac. Not Isaac.

*Please, Lord . . .*

"It's going to be okay," the man said. "I'm going to take care of everything."

His words caused bile to rise in her.

Madison forced her eyes open.

The man peering over her wasn't wearing a mask this time—only a camera strapped to his forehead.

The face that she saw sent chills through her.

---

# CHAPTER FIFTY-THREE

AS SHANE SAT at the conference room table, his gaze wandered to a file folder left by one of his colleagues. Various papers stuck out from the edges, mostly memos brought in from the field office.

He opened the folder, pulled out a few notes and began to flip through some agency updates, hoping if he focused on something else a moment he might think more clearly.

His gaze stopped on one of the memos.

A man charged with murdering his family had been released from the psychiatric ward where he was being treated. His crimes had been blamed on his medications, and he'd supposedly recovered and been cleared to resume life as normal.

Shane's eyes narrowed as he continued to read the details.

Wayne Cox.

Why did that guy's name sound familiar?

That's when he realized that Madison had mentioned him before.

Wayne's sister was one of Madison's clients at the nonprofit. Madison had helped this woman recover after her brother had killed the rest of her family. Based on everything Shane knew about the crime, the man was basically a psychopath. A brilliant psychopath but insane, nonetheless.

He stared at the man's face. His build. The slight hunch in his shoulders.

Something seemed familiar about him.

Shane's heart slowed as realization washed through him.

He remembered walking through Fog Lake with Madison and seeing the man wearing his hat pulled down low over his face.

His instincts had told him something was off about the guy.

Before he could investigate, the little boy had almost been hit and Shane had been distracted.

Could that man have been . . . Wayne?

Shane stared at the photo again.

It seemed a good possibility.

He needed to talk to Madison. Needed more information. He grabbed his phone and dialed her number.

But she didn't answer.

Unrest jostled inside him.

Madison not answering her phone might not mean anything.

Or it could mean everything.

---

"WHERE'S ISAAC?" Madison's voice wavered as the question left her lips.

"Doesn't matter. He's not important to me." The man peered down at her, a creepy smile on his face.

He was enjoying this, wasn't he?

Bile rose in her.

Why did this guy seem familiar? He was probably in his mid-twenties and of average height with dark hair cut short to the scalp. His obsidian eyes were hooded. A scar stretched across his cheek.

Still, Madison couldn't place him.

He wasn't anyone she'd suspected. Yet, he still seemed familiar.

A grin spread across his lips as he studied her face. "You still don't know who I am, do you?"

Madison tried to think, but her head pounded so hard. She touched her forehead and felt dried blood. That car accident had beaten her up pretty good. It had definitely left her in a weakened state.

That was exactly what this guy had wanted, wasn't it?

She glanced around, wondering where she was.

This man had laid her on a ratty brown couch. The wall of a log cabin stretched behind him. Flames danced in the fireplace across the room.

Darkness concealed the view out the window. But, if she had to guess, she was still close to Fog Lake, maybe in one of the cabins surrounding the town.

The place smelled old, like it hadn't been used in a while.

Was there anyone near that could help her?

"Where's Isaac?" Madison repeated, her gaze meeting the man's.

"Like I said, he's not important to me. But you are. I don't need him or anyone else interfering with my plans." Amusement stretched through his gaze. "So, I left him."

Another cry escaped her lips. "You just left him there? Is he okay?"

Images of her brother bleeding out filled her thoughts. What if Isaac was seriously injured? He needed help.

At least, he wasn't trapped here with her. Maybe that was a good thing. Maybe he had a better chance of survival.

But still . . .

"Don't worry about him," the man said. "Worry about yourself. Do you know who I am yet?"

Madison licked her dry lips, wishing she had that answer. But she still didn't. The ringing in her ears and the pounding in her head . . . she just couldn't think clearly.

"You're The Good Samaritan Killer?"

He stared at her until a chuckle emerged—a long, loud chuckle meant to make her feel small and stupid. "You ruined my life, you know."

"I've never seen you before."

He paced beside the couch where she lay. "I'm Wayne Cox."

At once, realization filled her.

Belinda's brother . . . the one who'd killed his family. The one who'd just been released . . .

"No . . ."

Satisfaction filled his gaze. "That's right. You recognize me now, huh? Thanks to you, my sister hates me."

Madison's thoughts raced as she tried to figure out how to respond. "I didn't tell her to hate you. I was just trying to help her get back on her feet after what you did."

"It wasn't my fault. I was out of my mind." The mocking tone to his voice proved he'd faked his medication issues. "But I'm all better now."

"Good, then you can let me go." Her throat burned as she said the words.

"What people don't know was that I didn't have a psychotic break. I'd killed before—I just hadn't been caught. After I killed the first time, I got a taste for it. A craving. That's why I did it again . . . and again."

She swallowed hard. "But why your family?"

He scoffed. "My *family* never believed in me. They thought I should be sent away. I heard them whispering. Heard them plotting against me. They never believed in me. They were going to try to admit me to a mental hospital. I couldn't let that happen."

"It wasn't an accident that Belinda wasn't home, was it?"

"Belinda was the only one who understood me. I

did it before she got home, almost as a favor. But she didn't appreciate it."

This man . . . he was sick. Beyond reason.

All Madison could do right now was try to buy time until someone found her.

"But what does all this have to do with me?" Madison tried to keep him talking.

"Belinda was the only person in my life who cared about me, and you made her turn against me. You made her hate me. You need to pay."

"Belinda made her own choices. I was there to help her. She was afraid of you."

"I would never hurt my sister! I wanted to *be* in Belinda's life." His gaze narrowed. "But because of you, that's not going to happen."

Based on the deranged look in his eyes, Madison wasn't sure if she'd be able to keep him talking long enough for help to arrive before it was too late.

# CHAPTER FIFTY-FOUR

BRAMMALL RUSHED into the conference room. "I found out something you're going to want to know."

Shane sat up straighter, hoping for good news. "What's going on?"

"Park rangers just came upon a traffic accident right outside of town. It was Isaac Colson's car."

Shane's breath caught. "And?"

"Isaac was inside. They say he'll be okay, but he went to the hospital for treatment."

His heart pounded. "And Madison?"

Brammall paused before saying, "She wasn't in the car."

Shane's heart beat even harder.

He knew what that meant.

The Good Samaritan Killer had gotten Madison.

Where was Madison now? Was she even still alive?

She *had* to be.

*Please, God . . .*

Shane stood and grabbed his keys. "I need to get to the hospital and talk to Isaac. See what he knows."

"That's what I thought," Brammall said. "I knew you'd want to know right away."

He had to hurry.

Because every second counted right now.

---

"WHAT ARE you going to do with me now?" Madison hardly wanted to ask the question. But she had, and now she dreaded hearing the answer.

Because she knew . . .

He was going to kill her.

"Wouldn't you like to know?" Something about the Wayne said the words made it clear he was going to enjoy himself whatever it was he was planning.

She couldn't think about that right now, though.

Madison had no choice but to focus on surviving instead of giving in to her fear. Any other option would end in certain death.

"You've been the one behind all these crimes?" Madison asked. "All because I helped your sister after the horrible things you did?"

Wayne stared at Madison, the amusement disappearing from his gaze, replaced with pure, unmistakable hatred. "That's right. You ruined my life, so I'm going to ruin yours. As soon as I learned who you were, I began doing all the research I could. I heard about what your father did."

"My father is innocent," Madison stated. Even in her injured state, her voice sounded hard and confident.

"It was fascinating—so fascinating. I began reading everything I could about the situation. Watching all the specials on TV. It was amazing what James Colson was able to accomplish before he was caught. Ironically, he was caught because of you. That's not a very loving daughter, is it?" The amused tone returned.

"So, you researched me, found that out, and decided to lure me back to Fog Lake?"

He chuckled, somehow managing to keep his sneer in the process. "Once I was released from Airedale, I began following you. Watching you."

If Madison remembered correctly, Airedale was

the psychiatric hospital where he'd been sent after being deemed unfit to stand trial.

"But why here? Why didn't you just kill me when you had the chance?"

"That would have been too quick. It's the time leading up to death that's frightening. You deserved to suffer. I knew if I wanted justice, I needed to get you back to Fog Lake, where it all began. What better way than by going after your aunt? By killing her like your dad killed those other women. It was brilliant, if you ask me."

"Verna was innocent in all this." Madison tried to sit up, but pangs shot through her head, and she sank back down.

Wayne shrugged as if he didn't care. "But was she? From what I understand, she didn't exactly treat you guys very well."

"She didn't deserve to die like that."

Wayne's gaze locked on hers. "Admit it. She got what she deserved."

Madison wasn't going to bother to respond to that.

"Now here you are—the perfect ending to my story."

Madison swallowed hard. She didn't even want

to begin thinking about where he was going with this.

She licked her lips. "What about those other women? Susan? Alexandria? Why pull them into this?"

"Susan caught my eye at the hotel when I saw her sending flirty looks to your brother. I knew she'd be perfect. And Alexandria . . . she was in your older brother's class. She had a special place in her heart for him, so I knew she'd be perfect also. Whatever I could do to turn your whole family upside down, that's what I wanted."

"You've succeeded. So, why can't you leave us alone now?"

His nostrils flared as he easily glided between emotions. "Because that wouldn't be any fun. That's not what The Good Samaritan Killer would have done."

"But you're *not* The Good Samaritan Killer."

His eyes glinted. "Maybe I could be."

The way he said the words made another chill wash through Madison.

She wasn't going to survive this, was she?

As if to confirm that thought, Wayne reached behind him and pulled a gun from his waistband.

# CHAPTER FIFTY-FIVE

SHANE STARED AT ISAAC, who lay in the hospital bed, his body just as wrecked as his car.

"I wish I could help you," Isaac muttered, his voice faint and weak. "But I don't know what else to say."

Shane's gut tightened. Isaac wasn't in any shape to talk. His head was bandaged. A cannula stretched beneath his nose. Cuts marred his face.

But time was of the essence right now.

"Can we just go through the details one more time?" Shane said. "Just to be certain?"

"Of course. Whatever you need." But Isaac's eyes drifted shut before flinging open again.

At any time, his pain medication could fully kick in, and Isaac would be totally useless.

"What's the last thing you remember?" Shane rushed.

Isaac squinted and touched the bandage across his head. "I wish I had more to tell you. But all I remember is riding down the road with Madison. We went around the corner, and all of a sudden this vehicle appeared in my lane. The lights were bright and blinding. I couldn't see anything. Before I could move out of the way, the driver slammed into us. Everything went black, and now here I am. I don't remember anything else. Believe me, I've tried."

Shane fisted his hand as he fought off his frustrations. He'd been hoping for more. Praying for more.

But he couldn't blame Isaac.

He was a victim in all this also.

Isaac's gaze latched onto his. "This guy has Madison, doesn't he? This is the work of The Good Samaritan Killer . . . or the man who's pretending to be."

Shane didn't deny his words. Instead, he nodded somberly. "I'm sorry. But it's the only thing that makes sense."

Isaac's lips twitched down into a frown. "Have any videos appeared yet?"

Shane glanced at his phone, checking for an

update. He'd been hoping to hear something from Brammall. But there was nothing.

He pulled his gaze back up to Isaac's. "We're watching for them. But, no, not yet."

"We've got to find this guy, Townsend." Isaac's voice cracked as his eyes latched onto Shane's, a burst of energy seeming to hit him. "You can't let him kill my sister."

Just hearing the words aloud made Shane's blood boil. "I don't intend on letting that happen. We're trying to track down the owner of the truck left at the scene. Apparently, it was stolen from a house in Gatlinburg last night. Does the name Wayne Cox mean anything to you?"

Isaac's eyes shifted back and forth with thought. "No, it doesn't. Why?"

"We believe the brother of one of the women Madison worked with may be behind this. It might be that he is bent on some type of revenge."

Isaac's face seemed to go paler. "I don't like the sound of that."

Shane bit down. "Neither do I."

"WHERE ARE WE?" Madison tried to keep Wayne talking, tried to buy some more time.

But was she just delaying the inevitable?

Probably.

Wayne twirled the gun on his finger, the safety pulled. One wrong move and . . .

But that was his point, wasn't it?

He wanted Madison to be afraid.

"It's not important where you are," he muttered. "No one will ever find you here. That's the only thing you need to know."

Her throat tightened at his words. What if he was right?

"There has to be another way." Her voice trembled.

"That's what a lot of people say before I kill them. Your father was very inspiring to me. Did I mention that?"

"Leave my father out of this." Madison's voice held a sharp edge. "He's innocent."

"Isn't it funny the way you think your father is innocent, and everyone else who's been sent to jail is guilty?"

Her jaw tightened at his accusation. "That's not the way it is."

"But isn't it?"

"What I'm trying to do is help people rebuild their lives. It doesn't matter if their loved one is guilty or not. What matters is the fact that people's lives have been turned upside down and they need help recovering."

"If Belinda had stuck by me, I wouldn't be in this position right now."

Madison licked her lips. "You have to own your choices. Nobody else can force you into them."

"You don't understand!" His nostrils flared again as his eyes widened.

Madison was making him angry. She needed to watch her words before he lashed out and did something irreversible. This was no time to stir up his emotions.

"You're right. I don't understand. I'm sorry." Her thoughts raced. "Why did you grab another woman —Alexandria? Where is she now?"

"She's alive."

Her breath caught. "What? Where?"

He smirked. "I left her at a park—to distract the feds so I could grab you, of course. Everything I did was for a purpose. Everything."

This man was a cold, calculated killer.

Madison's head swam. How was she going to get out of this?

She needed more time to figure out that answer.

She shifted, letting out a moan as she did. "Listen, could you get me some water? Please?"

He scoffed. "Why should I? You're just going to die anyway."

Her heart pounded harder. "I feel . . . faint. My mind is going in and out, and I can't think. My body . . . it's breaking down."

If she died on her own, where would the fun be? That's what she was banking on, at least.

Wayne stared at her a moment before stepping back. "I suppose I could get you some water."

As he strode away, Madison released her breath. Her mind raced.

How was she going to get out of this situation?

She glanced around, looking for anything she could use as a weapon. But as she shifted on the couch, her ribs ached. Every time she moved, more pain shot through her—sometimes in new areas. How many broken bones did she have?

Could she even walk?

There had to be a way she could escape.

She just needed to think a little harder.

And pray.

She needed to pray like her life depended on it . . . because it did.

# CHAPTER FIFTY-SIX

"WE HAVE ANOTHER VIDEO," Brammall announced as soon as Shane got back into the office.

Shane rushed toward the computer and leaned over Brammall, watching the footage over his shoulder.

From the very beginning, Shane felt nausea rising in him.

The footage showed someone from an immersive point of view running from his truck after he'd come upon the scene of an accident.

"This doesn't look good," the man muttered. "I think someone's inside."

The man opened the door, and Madison's face came into view. Blood ran down her forehead and cheeks. Her eyes were closed.

She'd lost consciousness.

The sight of her made Shane's heart pound harder.

At least, she'd survived the accident.

Isaac slumped in the driver's seat beside her, collapsed against the airbag.

"I've got to get you some help." The man took Madison's seatbelt off and lifted her from the car. As he carried her away, the video faded to black.

Shane assumed the footage was over, but the next instant, a new frame appeared.

This time, Madison lay on an old couch in a log cabin, resting with a blanket over her.

"I'm going to take good care of you, Madison," the man murmured. "Such good care of you."

Shane's stomach roiled again. What did the man mean by that?

He had no doubt it was nothing good.

SHANE WATCHED the video for probably the twentieth time. Each time, he tried to pick up on something that would give him a clue as to where Madison could be.

He'd even let Bear into the room to watch it also.

The man had grown up in the area. Maybe he had some insight.

He was desperate enough that he'd try anything at this point.

"You really care about her, don't you?" Bear's voice cut through the air.

Shane swung his head toward Bear, surprised at the question.

His first inclination was to deny the truth. But he wouldn't do that.

Instead, he scrubbed a hand over his beard and sighed. "I do. I had no intentions of it. But, in a short time, she's come to mean a lot to me."

"I can tell. I can see by the way she looks at you that she feels the same."

A rush of warmth filled him. He couldn't deny his feelings. But would he ever have a chance to tell Madison that she should give him a chance? That the two of them could overcome the obstacles in their lives together?

He ran a hand through his hair. "I want to find her, Bear. But . . . we have so little to go on here."

Bear frowned. "I know, I keep watching the video, hoping that something will pop out. But all these cabins around here seem to look the same."

"I've checked with a lot of the rental agencies,

but none of them know anything about this guy. I have people looking into him now. I'm just afraid that by the time we find the information we need, it will be too late."

"That thought has crossed my mind also." As Bear stared at the video, his breath caught. "Wait . . ."

"What is it?"

"Pause it there."

Shane did.

Bear pointed at the screen. "The wood in the log cabin . . . it looks like birch."

"What about it?"

"That's not a typical wood for cabins in this area. If I remember correctly, a developer built five or six rental cabins out of that wood about ten years ago. They were shut down last year because he'd apparently cut some corners. One of them caught on fire due to electrical issues, and this developer has been fighting to have them reopened since then."

Shane's heart beat faster. "Do you know where these cabins are?"

Bear pulled out his phone. "I can find out."

"Hurry. We don't have any time to waste."

Bear's lips flickered downward in a frown. "Believe me, I know."

# CHAPTER FIFTY-SEVEN

WAYNE GLANCED AT HIS WATCH, his lips flickering with impatience. "Take another sip of that water. Then we need to get moving."

Another shot of cold terror ripped through Madison. "What do you mean?"

"You're not stupid. You've got to know I have other plans for you. We have to get moving. Nothing can get in my way."

Her heart pounded in her ears. "What exactly is your plan?"

"Well, I suppose at this point it wouldn't hurt to tell you." He smiled, even though his eyes looked empty. "I have another car waiting outside. I'm going to put you in the driver's seat, start the engine, and then send you down the mountain. It won't be a fun way to go, but it's necessary."

Trembles overtook her body at the thought, at the realization of how much pain she might have to go through before this ended—in either life or death.

She hated feeling powerless to stop it.

Certainly, there was something she could do.

"None of this is necessary," she started. "You need help, Wayne. There are better ways to handle this ..."

"I'm tired of people telling me I need help!" he yelled. "I'm fine just the way I am. I just like getting my own sense of justice, and there's nothing wrong with that. If you'd minded your own business, we wouldn't be in this position right now."

Her lungs tightened with fear. "Wayne, let me call someone who can take you to the hospital. Maybe there's medication they can give you."

"I don't want medication. What I want is to finish what I started."

Before Madison could say anything else, he reached under her and lifted her from the couch. Pain ripped through her body.

But she was going to have to push through the hurt. If Wayne thought he was going to be able to do this without her putting up a fight, he was wrong.

At once, she began thrashing and kicking.

Wayne fell back, Madison still in his arms.

As they hit the floor, she rolled onto her hands and knees. She tried to crawl away, looking for anything that might protect her as she did.

"Oh, no, you don't." Wayne grabbed her leg and jerked her back toward him.

A scream caught in her throat as he towed her across the floor.

The next instant, he pinned her down.

"You're stronger than I thought you were," he muttered as he glared down at her.

He reached in his back pocket and pulled out a syringe. "But I have something that will make this easier on both of us."

***

"THEY'RE RIGHT HERE." Bear pointed to an area on the map to the west of town. "I'm certain of it."

It was something. Better than what they had before—which had been nothing.

"Let's go." Shane nodded to his colleagues to follow him.

Bear rose also and took a step after them.

Shane paused. "I'm not sure it's a good idea for you to go."

"Please." Bear's gaze latched onto his. "There's already been so much lost time between my sister and me. I can't lose her now. She needs me. Please."

Shane stared at him another second before nodding. He didn't have time to argue. They needed to get going.

Moments later, Shane was in his car with Brammall and Bear. Four other FBI agents were also in their vehicles. They would cut their lights before they pulled up to the cabins, not wanting to give anyone a heads-up they were coming.

Shane's heart pounded inside him. He hoped this would lead somewhere and wasn't for nothing.

Mostly, he prayed Madison was still okay. That they'd find her in time.

But so much felt uncertain right now.

"I have an update on this guy for you." Brammall looked at his phone. "We managed to get some of Wayne Cox's records from his therapist back in Minnesota. Turns out this guy was being treated for multiple mental health issues. He has some OCD on top of bipolar disorder and psychopathic tendencies."

This man sounded like exactly the kind of guy people should be terrified of.

Now he had Madison.

Why hadn't Shane thought earlier to look into these people connected with her job?

Finally, they reached the turnoff to the cabins. They cut their lights as they crept closer. As the buildings came into view, Shane saw one of the cabins had a faint glow coming through the windows.

Someone was inside.

It was the perfect location. Secluded. Out of the way. And currently not in use.

How had this guy even known about these cabins?

That was the least of Shane's concerns right now.

They pulled to the side of the road, and he drew his gun. Before he left his car, he glanced back at Bear one more time. "Stay here. The last thing we need is for you to get in our way. Especially since the situation is delicate."

Bear nodded. "Got it."

Shane climbed out and prayed that this would have a happy ending.

# CHAPTER FIFTY-EIGHT

MADISON SAW the needle and gasped. She knew that once Wayne injected her with that sedative—she assumed that's what it was—that she wouldn't stand a chance.

But how could she stop him?

Maybe someone was close enough to hear her call out. Probably not, but maybe. She had nothing to lose right now.

As he held up the syringe, Madison screamed.

Wayne's eyes widened, and his hand slapped her cheek.

Her skin stung—one more throb to add to an already long list.

"You shouldn't have done that," he muttered.

"You don't think I'm stupid enough to have brought you somewhere anyone could hear you, right?"

She spotted a hand-carved, wooden bear statue on the floor within reach.

As Wayne pushed the air from the syringe, Madison grabbed the decoration. She swung it, and the statue collided with his head.

Wayne fell to the floor. The syringe went flying across the floor and rolled under a piece of furniture. Madison wasted no time scrambling toward the door.

If she could just get outside . . .

This was her chance, maybe her *only* chance to live.

SHANE HEARD Madison's scream come from inside the house.

With his colleagues lined up on either side of the door, he gave them a nod before bursting into the house.

His eyes widened when he saw Madison reaching for the door.

Wayne stood behind her, blood dripping from a gash in his forehead, and a crazy look in his eyes as he held a gun in his hands—a gun aimed at Madison.

"Madison, get down!" Shane yelled.

Madison dropped to the floor.

As Wayne looked up and raised his gun, Shane fired.

Wayne clutched his chest as a spot of blood appeared.

A growing spot of blood.

The man collapsed to the ground.

As the other agents rushed toward Wayne, Shane knelt on the floor beside Madison and examined her. She had cuts and bruises on her face—from the accident he assumed—and she held her ribcage as if in pain.

She'd looked better—but she was still alive.

That's what mattered most.

Warmth and gratitude spread through his chest.

"Are you okay?" he rushed.

Madison nodded, her eyes glazed with exhaustion and pain. "I am now. How did you even find me?"

"You can thank Bear for that."

"And Isaac? Is he ... ?"

"He's at the hospital. I went and talked to him.

He's going to be okay. We have an ambulance on the way here now so someone can look at you too."

Madison nodded, seeming reassured now that her questions were answered.

She leaned into his chest and closed her eyes.

Shane wrapped an arm around her shoulders and pulled her closer, happy that this was all over ... finally.

# CHAPTER FIFTY-NINE

A WEEK LATER, Madison opened the door to the cabin of her childhood home and smiled at the person on the other side.

Special Agent Shane Townsend.

He stepped closer and dipped his head toward her. "Hey, there. How you feeling?"

She shrugged. "Progressing."

Three ribs were bruised. She had five stitches in her forehead and a concussion.

But all things considered, she counted herself fortunate.

"I'd say come in, but how about if we sit on the porch instead?"

"It's a beautiful day. I'd love to."

Bear had been helping her get this place cleaned

up. No longer was the word "Killer" slashed across the front of the cabin. The whole home had been power-washed. The boards had been taken off the windows and new curtains hung.

Madison was going to stick around here longer—until she had more resolution.

Because Wayne Cox was in jail.

But she wasn't convinced all this was over.

Isaac had gone back to Memphis, but he promised to come if Madison needed him. Alexandria had recovered and returned home. And Madison was now working remotely—at least, for now.

She and Shane settled beside each other on the porch swing and stared at the colorful mountains around them.

As they did, Shane reached into his pocket and pulled out a bag. "Cheddar and caramel popcorn?"

Madison grinned. "I'd love some."

She snatched a few kernels and popped them in her mouth.

As she did, she rested her head on Shane's shoulder. He slipped his fingers between hers, and they swung silently for several minutes.

"There's something I need to tell you," he started.

"What's that?"

"It's . . . about your dad."

Madison sat up, her back suddenly ramrod straight. "What about him? Is he okay?"

Shane nodded. "He's fine. I didn't mean to scare you. It's about . . . The Good Samaritan Killer."

He had her full attention now. "What's going on?"

He stared into the distance for a moment before turning back to her. "If I tell you something, I need you to promise to keep it between us."

"Of course."

"There's one detail about the murders fifteen years ago that the feds never released to the public."

Her heart pounded in her ears. "Okay . . ."

"This killer . . . he carved the initials GSK into his victims' skin, on the tender underside of their arm."

Instinctively, Madison reached for that area, trying to process what he'd told her.

"I'm still not sure where you're going with this."

He pressed his lips together, obviously burdened by this conversation. "Here's the thing. Even after your father was captured, this news was never shared. I didn't think much about it at first. But it's been bugging me ever since I came to Fog Lake."

"How?"

"If my father truly thought he put the right guy

behind bars, why would he keep that information hidden?"

Her mind raced. "What are you getting at, Shane?"

"The only reason I can come up with that he wouldn't share that information is because he wasn't sure if they had the right guy. He wanted to hold on to the fact just in case the real Good Samaritan Killer struck again."

The air left her lungs. "You really think that?"

"It's the only thing that makes sense."

"Have you told anyone?" she rushed.

"I can't. It's just a theory. I have no proof."

"But if that's true—"

He raised a hand, silently urging her to slow down. "I know. Believe me, I know. But I need to keep looking into this. I'm still concerned about the times your father left at night, the times he doesn't want to explain."

"I don't know why he won't offer an explanation." She shifted. "Why did you tell me about your doubts?"

He tilted his head closer. "Because I care about you, and I don't want to keep secrets. There are things I can't share because of my job but ..."

She reached for him and rested her hand on his

neck. Their foreheads connected as she leaned into him. "Are you going to look into it?"

"I am."

She reached up and planted a kiss on his lips. "Thank you."

With his lips less than an inch from hers, he murmured, "You're welcome."

"Does that mean you're going to be spending more time here in Fog Lake?"

"It looks like I will be."

She grinned at the thought of seeing him more. "I would like that. A lot."

"I was hoping you would."

~~~

If you enjoyed this book, please consider leaving a review!
~~~

COMING NEXT: SECRETS OF SHAME